Old Shadows, New Murder

Sharon McGregor

Whimsical Publications, LLC

Florida

Old Shadows, New Murder is a work of fiction. Names, characters, and incidents are the products of the author's imagination and are either fictitious or are used fictitiously. Any resemblance to actual events or persons, living or dead, is entirely coincidental.

To purchase the authorized electronic edition of
Old Shadows, New Murder, visit
www.whimsicalpublications.com

Cover art by Traci Markou
Editing by Destiny Booze

ISBN-13: 978-1-940707-54-9

Published by
Whimsical Publications, LLC
Florida

Acknowledgement

To everyone who has lived in a small town,
or wished they did.

Taylor set the journal aside and put the lot of them in a box she'd started to fill with ornaments. She would try to get back to them tomorrow, but now it was time to take care of supper. Denver had begun to wrap himself around her ankles, and Tristan was making snuffling noises as he did when he was getting hungry.

It would be an early bedtime tonight. She was strangely tired, and she hadn't really done that much. Maybe it was aftershock. It was only the day before yesterday they had buried Aunt Grace, but it seemed eons ago.

She lay in bed, feeling terribly tired but not able to sleep. She finally gave up and turned on the light, pulling an old Agatha Christie from the bookshelf—Aunt Grace's favorite author. She'd read them all, but maybe that's what she needed to lull herself to sleep, something familiar. It worked. Twenty minutes later, she turned out the light and drifted off.

She awoke in the dark to a low growling coming from Tristan. Then he gave a couple of short woofs and grabbed the covers, pulling them from the bed. Taylor sat up quickly. She heard someone moving in the house. It was coming from the attic. Tristan was now scratching at the door to get out.

"No way," Taylor whispered. "Whoever's there is probably bigger than me and certainly bigger than you. Sh. Be quiet."

Her cell phone was charging on the bedside table. Thank heavens she hadn't left it downstairs. She dialed 9-1-1 and then realized Badger Lake wasn't set up for the 9-1-1 service. She didn't know the police number by heart, and probably no one would be there in the night anyhow. The only number she knew was Edie's. She hated to wake her and alarm her, but she wasn't about to leave this room. She dialed. Edie's voice answered, surprisingly awake.

She whispered as loudly as she dared "Edie, can you call the police? There's someone in the house. I think they're in the attic."

"Hang up."

She did, and it was only minutes later that she saw lights flashing through her window—car lights. No siren, but whoever was upstairs knew it was time to leave. She heard a clatter in the hallway from someone half-falling down the ladder and footsteps racing downstairs. The lights flashed again and disappeared.

About ten minutes later, there was a knock on the door

and a loud voice said, "Taylor? It's Sergeant Scott. I'm coming in. The door's open."

By now, she had managed to climb into some jeans and a sweatshirt. She met him at the bottom of the stairs.

"You didn't leave your door unlocked?"

"No, of course not. I always lock up."

He looked down at her from his considerable height advantage and said in a skeptical tone, "There's no sign of a break-in. The door is quite intact."

"That may be, but I locked the door. Someone must have broken in somehow." No six-foot-plus cop in cowboy boots and jeans was going to intimidate her. Then she gave a guilty start.

"Yes?" he prompted.

"Aunt Grace used to leave a spare key hidden outside in case she was ever locked out, and I just left it there."

"Let me guess," he said. "Under a flower pot?" He nudged a container of desiccated begonia blooms with his toe, and a key on a red ring appeared. "I imagine there are probably about two people in Badger Lake that don't know where she hides the key." Then he smiled, and she forgave him for the slights on her security breach. His smile had the melting power of a warm Calgary Chinook. Now where did that come from? Taylor was not normally prone to flights of fancy.

She remembered her manners. No matter what time of day or night, Aunt Grace would never leave someone on the doorstep without an offer of nourishment. "Would you like a cup of coffee?"

"I'd love one, but I think, right now, we both need sleep. I do need to get some details from you for my report. If I come by tomorrow morning around ten, will you still offer me coffee?"

"I might even find a cookie to go with it."

"I'll just take a quick look to be sure everything is all right. I tried to follow the guy around the back, but, with not much in the way of streetlights, he slipped off into the dark." The sergeant disappeared up the stairs followed by Tristan, and she heard him pulling the ladder up again. Back downstairs, he handed her the key, and said, "Best keep this inside now." And he backed out of the driveway with a little flutter of gravel.

Chapter One

She placed her foot on the first rung of the ladder. She felt them all staring at her, waiting for her to fail. She would show them she was able to do anything they could. She would prove she belonged. She would prove to him she belonged. Another foot, another rung. She ignored the inner voice that told her to change direction, to move her foot downward to the lower rung instead of climbing higher. Her heart raced, fluttering as though trying to escape her chest.

Taylor turned the key in the old-fashioned lock and pushed the door open. It groaned a little before stretching far enough for her to glimpse the outline of the huge fridge that dominated the opposite wall, the shadows giving it an added bulk. She wrinkled her nose, trying to decipher the smells—stale food, strong cleaners, musty old house, and the scent of past lives. She shivered a little as she imagined the sound of tiny creatures scurrying for shelter. Quickly, she turned on the light, and the room lost its eeriness. Her Jack Russell, Tristan, ran barking into the house, sniffing corners, and chasing away any bogeymen the light might have missed.

Now the house took on the familiarity she had felt years ago when she and her older brother, Greg, had lived here with their aunt. The old fridge was still the same one they had rummaged in for after school snacks, never sure what they would find. Aunt Grace had not been the best cook or housekeeper. The stove was new, comparatively, but the elements were grungy, and she knew better than to examine the stovetop sides for streaks of grease and heaven knew what else. She automatically checked the garbage bin, but it was empty. The odors didn't come from there. They were ingrained into every pore of the house, and nothing but a deep scouring of all surfaces would eradicate them. The house had sat empty for two weeks now, since Aunt Grace had first gone into the hospital.

The last few times Taylor had visited home, she couldn't help noticing the decline in Aunt Grace's abilities. She had only been in her sixties, but her eyesight had been failing, and she probably hadn't seen a lot of the grime that filled the corners.

Taylor sighed and tried to turn her thoughts in other directions. That line brought too strong a feeling of guilt. She should have come home more, especially after Greg had died.

There wasn't time to worry about cleaning tonight. Instead, she would see if she could find the makings for tea and toast and then head to bed early. There was bread and frozen entrees in the freezer and margarine and marmalade in the fridge. Other than that, the fridge was empty. Taylor knew the good ladies of Badger Lake had come over and cleaned out the spoiled food while Aunt Grace had been in the hospital.

Naturally, there would be tea, cartons and cartons of it, in the cupboard next to the stove. If Armageddon ever loomed, Aunt Grace would never have run out of tea.

Taylor moved her cat, Denver, into the house with his food dishes and litter box. Tristan settled for a pee in the backyard and then ignored his kibble, eyeing her toast until she gave him some.

She turned on the TV to scare away the heavy silence and found an old Britcom on public television. She ran a cloth over the coffee table and pulled her feet under her—tabby cat on one side and Jack Russell on the other—while she ate her late supper and watched Judi Dench hiccupping her way through a wedding ceremony.

Chapter Two

He could stop her if he really tried. He could say, "No, don't do it. It doesn't matter to me." She might come down. But he looked at her face. It was so fixed, so determined, and he thought he'd lost the chance to connect. The others were concentrating so hard on the lonely figure he thought maybe, by will alone, they could make her continue. He felt suddenly ashamed. And afraid. It was out of hand now. He should have stopped it before it started.

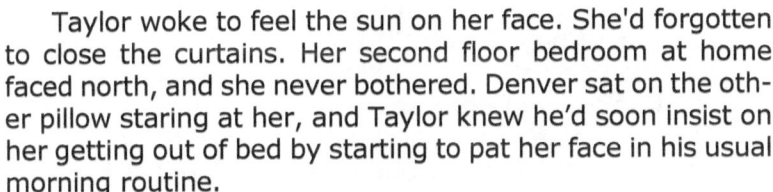

Taylor woke to feel the sun on her face. She'd forgotten to close the curtains. Her second floor bedroom at home faced north, and she never bothered. Denver sat on the other pillow staring at her, and Taylor knew he'd soon insist on her getting out of bed by starting to pat her face in his usual morning routine.

It wasn't long before Tristan began to whimper. Taylor needed a bathroom too, but Tristan came first. "Lucky you," she said to Denver. "I wish you could train Tristan to use your box."

The funeral wasn't till two. She'd gone over all the arrangements by phone with the funeral director and minister, but she still needed to be at the church by one, ahead of everyone else. The turnout would be a large one, she knew. Grace had lived here her whole life and worked in the town office for years. Everyone knew her. Small town funerals were a great social occasion. No one would leave before the lunch. It looked like it was going to be a beautiful autumn day, a great day for a funeral. Only farmers who might not be done harvesting wouldn't be there. Nothing stood between a sunny day and a farmer's combine when it was harvest time.

The United Church sat on a large lot at the edge of town. It was a new building, not the smaller one at the end of Main Street where Taylor and Greg had gone to Sunday school. Aunt Grace had never been much of a churchgoer. She had belonged to the Ladies' Aid and made a regular donation to the church, but said she had better things to do on Sunday. When Taylor had asked her why, she had said, "I do my part with the L.A., and I give them money for missionaries. I don't see how it will help them to see my aching butt on those hard pews every Sunday, just being able to fall asleep about the time the sermon ends. I'm sure God's not that interested in what I do on Sunday mornings." She had, however, felt it her duty to be sure Greg and Taylor had made it to Sunday school every week. She'd cleaned them up Sunday mornings and had handed them a tissue and an offering for the plate. When they had gotten home, she'd ask them what they'd learned that day. They'd said, "nothing much" and that had been it until next Sunday.

As she sat in the mourners' room off the church lobby, Taylor felt overwhelmingly alone. She was the only family member left to mourn her aunt's passing. Greg should have been with her. She didn't want to sit in the front pew alone on display. She knew all eyes would be on her, wondering about Greg and where her father was or even if he was still alive.

She cleared her throat and the funeral director, Mr. Evans, looked up inquiringly. She shook her head at him and glanced at the lobby. She saw some familiar faces and some not so. Then she saw one that was very familiar—a short, stocky woman with blunt-cut gray hair who was carrying, rather than using, a cane. Edie. She slipped out the door into the lobby and accosted her.

"Edie, would you sit with me? Please? You were her best friend. You should be in the mourners' section."

Edie glanced around and quickly said, "Of course, Taylor, if you want me to."

She led her back into the little side room.

"I'm sorry," Edie began.

"Me too," said Taylor. "You were closer to her than anyone. You're practically family."

Edie gave her a studied look but said no more. She just squeezed Taylor's hand.

Mr. Evans stood and said, "It's time now."

The casket was wheeled to the center aisle, and they followed it down the sloping carpet to the front pews. Evans motioned them to the right side and then took a seat on the left. The congregation remained standing as the organ began the strains of "Abide with Me." Taylor had left the hymn choices to the minister. She wrote the eulogy, but passed on the idea of standing to read it herself. At least he hadn't chosen "Amazing Grace" as the opening hymn, Taylor thought with a nervous giggle stuck in her throat. As she forced it away, the tears began to form in her eyes. In turn, she pushed them back. If someone had asked her later what the rest of the service consisted of, she would have been unable to answer, except for the eulogy, of course. It all passed in a dream.

Everyone filed past her after the service, sharing their condolences and memories of Grace. After a little lull, a couple she recognized as Bill and Evelyn Waters stopped in front of her. They were a Mutt and Jeff couple. Bill was a short, bustling man who looked as though he had an electric current running through him, and his wife, Evelyn, was a tall, slim, serene-faced woman who, it seemed to Taylor, had a difficult time keeping her serenity living with Bill.

Bill didn't offer to shake hands. Instead, he looked at her and said, "She'll be with God now." Religious statements always made Taylor feel a little awkward, and she didn't know how to answer. She remembered Bill was one of the Waters brothers who frequented the evangelical church and displayed behavior to suggest he had a volatile and emotional relationship with God. Bill apparently wasn't expecting an answer. He went on. "Not like your brother, Greg. He burned his bridges years ago, and now he'll be burning." As Taylor's mouth dropped, Evelyn shooed Bill away, whispering low to him, then throwing an apologetic smile over her shoulder toward Taylor.

The funeral director—she couldn't even remember his name—what was it? Stephenson, something like that. No, Evans, that was it. He took her arm to guide her to the waiting car to make the trip to the cemetery. Taylor didn't want to travel alone and gave Edie a pleading look. Edie never hesitated. She slid into the sleek, black mourners' car beside her.

Taylor wanted to ask Edie what she thought of Bill's comment or even if she had heard it, but now was not the time. What could Bill Waters have had against Greg, or know about her brother? Greg had left home when he was eighteen and, unlike Taylor, had rarely returned for visits.

Very few people attended the graveside part of the service. It was a long drive, and most of the crowd would already be queuing up in the church meeting room, making small talk and waiting for the first trays of sandwiches. The smell of coffee wafted over from the lunch room just off the church. The usually welcome smell twisted at Taylor's stomach.

Aunt Grace's burial site was an old family plot in a small cemetery about ten miles from Badger Lake. It was a silent drive there, and only three vehicles pulled to the side of the road in front of the old gate that had been swung open to accommodate them. The cemetery had only a few new graves. A lot of the stones were old and crumbling. A slightly newer section stood on a raised plateau in the back behind a stand of trees, but even that looked forgotten. A small building occupied center stage on the north side, the domain of the caretaker who made occasional swings by with a lawn mower. Families had moved away, next generations were intending to be buried in the new cemetery outside Badger Lake, and some of the names of long ago pioneers were probably now forgotten.

There were a few slots left in their family plot. Taylor's grandparents were there, a great-uncle or two, and a small baby grave sat in one corner. Taylor tried not to look at the marker that held Greg's name. She also tried not to look at her mother's. The empty spot beside her grave meant for Taylor's father would likely never be filled.

Now Aunt Grace was lowered into the ground and the few ceremonial handfuls of dirt followed her. It was all over, well, for Aunt Grace anyway. Taylor knew things were just beginning for her to tend to the aftermath of death.

Taylor felt conspicuously alone at the funeral luncheon, although she was surrounded by people stopping to pay their respects and fill their curiosity wells. Edie had slipped away shortly after they'd arrived back at the church.

Jack Vandenberg was one of the first. He loomed over Taylor, filling the standing room at the table's end. Jack had always been big, and the sort not easy to miss, even at school. Then he had been solid muscle honed by participating in every sport provided, especially football. Now his muscle was decidedly less firm, and he was slightly overflowing his belt. His hair was still outdoor-blond, but there was a noticeable sparseness over his forehead. He had left his coffee at the table, but was still clutching a paper plate stacked with Nanaimo bars and a lemon slice. "I know this isn't the time or place," he said. "But I would like to talk to you soon. Maybe I can call tomorrow?" Taylor knew Jack owned a local real estate company along with his father, but, even for him, this sounded a little pushy. She made a noncommittal murmur and passed her glance on to the person beside him.

Jenny Sandowski, or Jenny Bingham as Taylor remembered her, sat down beside her and greeted her as an old friend for a social occasion. They hadn't been friends that Taylor remembered. Jack and Jenny were a couple of years older than her. She remembered them hanging out with Greg and totally scorning her. Jenny was dressed in a pale yellow pant suit that fit her perfectly, a stark contrast to the funereal dark colors most of the others wore. She looked a far cry from the tomboy who had loved to climb and had excelled at gymnastics. Then she hadn't seemed to care much about what she'd worn. Now, she outshone everyone in the room, perhaps a strange result at a funeral. She made a few desultory comments about the attendance and the service and slipped away.

Bill and Evelyn Waters sat at a far table, and Taylor hoped they would stay there. They didn't. As they stopped beside Taylor, Bill remained silent and unusually still. It was Evelyn who spoke in her quiet voice. "We're so sorry about Grace," she said. "She was a big part of our town, and everyone will surely miss her. It's so sad when someone dies young."

Taylor had never considered her aunt's age from the viewpoint of a different generation, but she thought sixty-eight probably did seem young to the Waters.

"I hope we'll see more of you in the next while," Evelyn continued. "Are you planning to stay in Badger Lake?"

"I haven't made any plans yet." Taylor had no intentions of staying in Badger Lake, but she wasn't about to tell the Waters that. Anything she did say would be up for discussion in lunch and coffee conversations for the next week.

She couldn't wait to get out of this stifling church lunch

room. Finally, the last hangers-on decided they had homes to go to, and Taylor looked for the minister and Mr. Evans to see if there were any final things she needed to do. The funeral director had all the checks and honorariums ready for her. He gave her a binder with the cards from the flowers, the sympathy cards, and a list of addresses for the people she would have to send thank you notes to.

Now that Taylor could go, she had hoped to see Edie still there. Maybe she could give her a ride home. She wanted to ask her if she knew what Bill Waters had been talking about earlier with his comment about Greg. But there was no sign of Edie, so she headed back to the house alone. Tristan would need a walk, and Denver would be ready with his starving cat look.

She flipped her cell phone on again and saw the voice message alert flashing. She hit play. "Hello, Taylor, it's Melvin Donovan calling. Can you give me a call back when things have settled down? I have your aunt's will, and I'd like to go over it with you. I don't know how long you're planning to stay this time. Please call me."

Stay this time? What did he mean by that? Taylor's guilt immediately kicked in. She wondered if everyone thought she had neglected her aunt.

She called back. *Might as well get it over with.*

He answered. "Thanks for calling back, Taylor. I didn't know if you wanted to take care of things now, or if you wanted to wait till you come up for good. I know you must be busy."

"For good?"

"Sorry. I guess I'm making assumptions. I thought, well, never mind what I thought. Can you come by the office tomorrow morning around eleven? We can go over the terms of the will then."

"Eleven will be fine."

Tomorrow she could officially hear the terms of the will and then get started on cleaning up the house and getting it ready for market. She knew Aunt Grace had left the house to her and that she was executor along with the lawyer. She wanted to go talk to the other real estate agent, not the company that Jack Vandenberg owned. She'd never liked Jack much, even when they were kids, and he'd really crossed the line at the funeral. Actually, she hadn't liked any of Greg's friends that much. Maybe it was because they all conspired to keep her from tagging along on their adventures. They had been a funny crew. They'd called themselves The Famous Four. Jack was the jock, Jenny the female version of a jock, Tara Leigh had been the leader, socially clever but limited academically, and Greg had been the quiet, serious one. She wondered what they had all seen in each other to form such firm ties, but the friendships had held through their school years. Then it ended as they went their separate ways. Jack and Jenny probably saw each other, as they both stayed in Badger Lake, but she'd never heard Greg mention any of them after he'd moved. Then she remembered Rebecca Waters, Bill and Evelyn's daughter. She hadn't really been part of the group, but she'd hung around them from time to time. That brought back Bill Waters' comment, and she wondered about the connection.

Taylor needed to shop for supplies. Tea, toast, and marmalade were losing their charm after serving as both supper and breakfast. Besides, she was getting a coffee withdrawal headache. She should have had coffee at the luncheon instead of tea. She didn't want to shop at the local IGA or Co-op today when the funeral was fresh on everyone's mind. Maybe she could get a takeout coffee at the Subway on the edge of town and find a frozen dinner for tonight. She knew Aunt Grace's freezer would be full of one serving frozen entrees. Luckily, Tristan and Denver were well supplied. Shopping could wait till tomorrow. She turned the car toward Subway.

Later, she took Tristan for a short walk. The house was on the edge of town, or had been once. Now an apartment building for seniors and a residential care home filled the area where the old creamery used to be. The empty building once functioned as a sort of playground. It was supposedly locked and off limits, but that never stopped determined children, just made it more fun. Greg and his friends hung out there a lot. It had been kind of a clubhouse for them.

Past that was the road leading to the town cemetery, not the one where Grace was buried, but a larger, newer one. Then a track to the "nuisance grounds," as everyone called the local landfill.

On the way back, Taylor stopped to consider the second lot attached to the house. Aunt Grace had owned that too and had once bred border collies in a kennel she'd built there. In later years, she had turned it into a boarding kennel. She wondered if she ever had enough customers to fill it. Any time she'd come for a visit, there had usually only been one or two dogs boarded, but Taylor suspected her aunt had done it for the love of having dogs around her, not to make a real living at it. She'd been retired from the town office by then and needed to fill a void, Taylor guessed.

Now that the mechanics of the funeral were over, the loss Taylor felt over the passing of her last family member suddenly surfaced. She remembered Aunt Grace fussing over her dogs as she'd once fussed over her and Greg, not really an expert at parenting, but loving them all the same. Their mealtimes might have been haphazard, but they always knew if they needed a cry or a kind word of encouragement, Aunt Grace always knew what to do. Taylor's eyes began to fill, and by the time she opened the kitchen door, she found herself crying out loud. She threw herself on the couch and let the sobs come, washing out her sorrow and guilt and polishing her memories.

Chapter Three

She put one foot on the next rung of the ladder, trying to slow her breathing. She didn't want to hyperventilate. She heard them, as though through a thick door, urging her on. She took another step. She could turn around now. She could turn around and say no. She wouldn't do this. It was the only sane thing to do. She lifted her foot to climb down one rung, but it moved upwards instead, all on its own. After all, they had done it, so could she. She just had to get through this. Then they would see. Then she would show them she could do anything they could.

Just before eleven the next morning, Taylor opened the wood and glass door of Donovan Law Office. She walked up the creaky steps to the old fashioned office on the second floor. Melvin Donovan was waiting for her and ushered her inside, offering her coffee, which she gladly accepted, and a doughnut, which she refused. Somehow, wiping sugar glaze from your fingers and chin didn't seem to fit her idea of listening to a will reading.

"We're just waiting for Edie," he said. Taylor must have shown her surprise because he added, "The other beneficiary."

She heard footsteps approaching and had no time to ask questions. A moment later, Edie was installed in the seat beside her.

Melvin Donovan laid out the simple terms of the will. Taylor was to inherit the house and any remaining assets except for the lot with the kennel. That was left to Edie. There would be no problems separating the properties as the lots held their own titles.

In ten minutes or less, the meeting was over, and Taylor and Edie came out into the bright sunshine of an autumn day.

"Walk with me?" asked Edie.

"Of course." Edie only lived a block away from Aunt Grace's house. "Why don't you come in for tea?" she asked.

As Taylor fussed about the kitchen making tea and searching for packaged cookies, Edie suggested, "Top right cupboard are macaroons. You must be wondering about the will."

"Not really. You were her best friend, and I remember you always used to help her with the kennel even before she turned it into a boarding one. It's only natural." Actually, Taylor had been wondering, but she wasn't going to admit it to Edie.

"It's more than that, and I think maybe you already have had some inkling. I'm pretty sure most of Badger Lake has."

Taylor stopped in mid-step. She set the plate of cookies on the table, trying not to make eye contact with Edie. She was afraid if she looked up, her expression would give away her thoughts. "I don't know what you mean."

"Didn't you ever wonder why Grace never dated or showed any interest in men?"

"I thought she was just too busy looking after Greg and me."

"Ah, the self-centeredness of children. You never thought your aunt might have a personal life beyond you. Well, she did. We did."

Taylor flushed and wasn't sure why she found this so embarrassing. If Melvin Donovan had told her he'd had a secret relationship with Grace for years, would she feel the same? Probably not.

"I honestly had no idea."

"Does it bother you a lot, the thought of your aunt and me loving each other?"

Taylor cringed at the word "loving." All her life Edie had felt like part of the family, but not in that way. It just wasn't the type of relationship you expected in a small town. Or in your own family.

"It's just that I had no idea."

Edie stood up. "I'd better get home and look after Jasper," she said, referring to her golden retriever that once belonged to Aunt Grace. "I'll talk to you later."

"No, please sit down, Edie. I'm not being judgmental. I'm not. I just need to process the idea."

"And you need to be alone to think. I just wanted you to know how things were between Grace and me."

"That's why you looked so strange when I asked you to sit in the mourners' section. You wondered what people would think."

"Only for a second. That's all the time I usually give to what other people think."

That comment was so true it made Taylor smile.

"I'll talk to you tomorrow. Why not meet me for coffee at The Northland? Say ten-thirty?"

She was out the door surprisingly quick for a seventy-year-old woman who walked with a cane. Taylor sat at the kitchen table and tried to assimilate the information she'd just received. It was hard to imagine a lesbian relationship going undiscovered in a small town where everyone knew everyone else's business. But was it undiscovered? There was a good chance that everyone, well everyone but her, knew about it for years. Both Edie and Grace had lived all their lives in Badger Lake and had earned the respect of the town through their work in all aspects of town life. Small towns had probably the same percentage of gay relationships as cities. It's just that they didn't take as kindly to anything their parents or grandparents hadn't accepted. Gay rights and gay marriage were something they just never thought about. It didn't mean the relationship wasn't accepted. It just meant that it was never acknowledged verbally, therefore it didn't really exist and didn't need to be accepted or rejected. She shook her head. That was making it too complicated. The simple truth was Aunt Grace had had a longstanding, loving relationship with Edie, a woman she liked and respect-ed. What was there not to accept? She'd have to work on that. Right now, Tristan needed a walk, and then she had to go shopping. She'd think about Grace and Edie tonight.

She took Tristan for a walk around the town perimeter, again marvelling at the changes in the town. When she'd come up to visit Aunt Grace, her visits had centered on shopping, having tea in the backyard, and playing Chinese checkers or dominoes. She hadn't paid much attention to the rest of the town. Now, she noticed other changes besides the new church. There were whole rows of new builds, a few derelict houses and empty lots, some homes with real estate signs on them. She was glad to see there weren't too many. That boded well for her sale of the house. Badger Lake seemed to have fared well compared to other small towns that faced shrinkage and death as younger generations looked for better amenities. But then Badger Lake had the advantage of being on the cross of two highways, close to a large man-made lake with fishing and tourism prospects, and in the winter, there was a ski hill close by. Those probably kept the town viable. She wondered what Edie planned to do with the other lot and the kennel. It seemed a lot of work for little return to keep it going as a boarding kennel. But then Edie was never one to turn down a challenge. *Edie.* Now her thoughts turned back to Edie and Aunt Grace. Why had she never noticed anything? How was this knowledge going to affect the way she felt about Edie? What had it been like to try to keep their relationship under wraps? Too many questions. She'd think about them later.

Tristan grudgingly turned into the backyard. Walks were never long enough for him. She let him off the leash, and he chased flies around the yard for a while, stopping to sniff at clusters of weeds and grass. Taylor looked around with a sinking heart. There was more work to be done here than in the house. The old shed at the back was padlocked. She knew it held an old well, but heaven only knew what else it contained. The garden needed tending, the bushes trimmed and some dug up, and that monstrosity of a shed taken down. She tugged at the door to see if it would open, but it held fast. She would have to find the key, or have someone break into it.

When her grandparents lived here, the house had been outside the town limits and on its own septic system and well. Once the town expanded its services, the well had been covered, but the shed still stood. There were probably some gardening tools in there. Taylor couldn't remember ever looking or playing in there. It had been off limits because of the old well. Why hadn't they filled it in instead of just covering and hiding it? That's what she'd have to do now.

IGA wasn't too busy. She filled her cart quickly, hoping to get through the checkout before meeting anyone she knew. In front of the pet food section, she nearly bumped into Jack Vandenberg. He had an empty cart. She wondered if he was really shopping or just scouting for her.

"It's lucky I ran into you," he said. "Saves me stopping by. I tried your phone a few times, but no one answered, and Grace never got an answering service."

"I've been out," she said. If she had been home and seen his number on display, she probably wouldn't have answered anyhow.

"Do you think we could have coffee and discuss your plans for the house?"

"I really have to get these groceries home."

He scanned her cart. "Nothing there that will spoil."

"Look, Jack, I'm not ready to talk about selling the house yet. I haven't decided what to do about it yet. I may just decide to stay on." Taylor had no intentions of staying on, but it might work as a ploy to put Jack off for a while.

Taylor was sure real estate agents trained themselves to never show surprise, but she could have sworn Jack's jaw dropped slightly. It made her want to giggle. Badger Lake was making her revert to childish reactions.

"Whatever would you do in Badger Lake?" he asked. "Don't you have a job?"

"My job follows me, and as long as I have an Internet connection, I'm in business." She wasn't about to give him details on her work. Impertinent questions had always been her problem, but she didn't like them when they were directed toward her.

"I'm sure Badger Lake would start to bore you pretty quickly."

"I don't think so. And, whatever I do, it will be in my own good time. I have a lot of work to do on the place first, whichever way I decide."

"Work?"

"Yes. You, of all people, should know it's not in any shape to sell as it is."

"Oh, I think I could get you an as-is sale pretty quickly," he said. "Save you a lot of bother."

Taylor was quickly tiring of this conversation. "I'll let you know, Jack." And she began pushing her cart past him to signal the conversation was over.

When she rounded the corner to the cashier, she saw him in her peripheral sight. He was standing where she had left him, a thoughtful expression on his face as he looked in her direction. She avoided eye contact and started to put her purchases on the rolling counter.

After she had put the groceries away, she changed into some old jeans and a stained white tee and started the grungy business of cleaning the kitchen. After a couple of hours, Tristan and Denver decided she'd been ignoring them long enough and began to demand attention.

After another short walk for Tristan, Taylor cuddled with Denver as she had her afternoon tea. She decided a different course of work was in order. There was an old attic with a pull down ladder in the upstairs hallway, and she guessed that would need clearing out too. It would be a change from soaking her hands in cleaner and bleach.

The attic had been ignored for years. Taylor could tell by the clouds of dust that accompanied the ladder she pulled down. She listened for sounds of scurrying feet, and, hearing none, she began to climb. Hopefully, the news was out on the rodent grapevine that a dog and cat were in the residence, not that she ever knew of Aunt Grace having problems. She thought, a little too late, she should have brought a flashlight, but there was a string dangling from the ceiling. Wonder of wonders, when she pulled it, a dull light came on. There were still too many shadows to see clearly, but Taylor could make out old furniture pieces, some broken and some still probably usable, a couple of stand-up lamps, then boxes and boxes of who knew what.

She opened the nearest box and sneezed from the dislodged dust. There were books inside. Another box held more books. They looked old, maybe not salable, probably no collectible first editions amongst them. A few more boxes had old dishes and ornaments in them. She pulled a rearing horse out of one box. She remembered it from when she was little. It had stood on her bedside table. She'd named it Trigger after Roy Roger's horse because it was a palomino. Oh dear, this was going to take more work than she'd imagined. The furniture could be sorted into broken, which could just go to the nuisance grounds, or usable, which could be sold. The boxes of books could be sold, too, if anyone wanted them, or maybe she could donate them to the residential care home library. Maybe some of the old titles would bring back memories for the seniors. She really needed to wait till she decided what to do with the house to see if she wanted to sell all the downstairs furniture as well.

Taylor stopped herself there. *Wait till I decide what to do?* Where did that come from? She was going to sell the house and move back to her own apartment. The conversation with Jack must have put the idea of staying in her mind, and it certainly wasn't a realistic one. She had a life to return to. A life of sorts, anyhow. Then she wondered how much she would actually miss her old life if she didn't return. Her two-year relationship with Jonah had ended just before Aunt Grace's illness, and her closest friend had moved across the country when her husband's job changed. She felt more ties to Badger Lake than to her little apartment on a busy city street. Still, she couldn't picture staying here. As Jack had said, she'd be bored in a week.

She opened one more box and recognized Greg's handwriting on the front of an old blue scribbler labeled "Greg's Journal." Underneath was another red one marked the same, and another beneath that one. She remembered Greg had always kept a journal. She used to tease him about it and had told him only girls kept diaries. He had just ignored her as he had usually done and had gone on writing. She closed the lid again. Too many memories. The happy ones from their years in this house were too quickly followed by the pain that came later. She'd leave the attic for another day.

She was still brushing dust and cobwebs from her hair when she heard a knock at the door. She peered around the corner at the windowed top of the door. If it was Jack Vandenberg, she had no intention of answering. But Tristan began to bark, and she knew she'd lost that decision. Dogs were a great comfort when she felt nervous being alone, but not much help when she wanted to be that way.

It wasn't Jack at the door. It was Jenny Bingham, Jenny Sandowski now. She took a quick look at her watch. It was nearly six o'clock, a strange time for a visit. But then, Jenny had never been conventional.

"Come in, Jenny." She couldn't keep the note of surprise out of her voice. Jenny didn't seem to notice. She was already on her way in.

Jenny gave a look around the house before taking an offered seat in the living room. She sat down carefully on the edge of the chair, as if fearful of contaminants, crossed one trouser-clad leg over the other, and leaned forward. She was dressed casually in a coral-colored top and white pants. They suited her to perfection. Taylor was pretty sure the labels were ones she wasn't used to. The manicure probably didn't come cheaply either. Taylor cupped her hands defensively to hide her chipped nails and torn cuticles. She felt at a disadvantage. This well-turned version of Jenny was a contrast to the younger version that had hung around with her brother and had been into sports. Back then, Jenny had spent most of her time in jeans and runners—designer jeans and expensive runners, so maybe it wasn't such a stretch.

"Would you like some tea?" Taylor asked. Then, remembering her now stocked cupboards, added, "Or coffee?" Aunt Grace would never have asked a visitor, she would simply have put the kettle on.

"No thanks," said Jenny. "I only have a moment." She waited till Taylor sat down then started explaining the reason for her visit. "I was wondering if you'd decided what to do about the house yet?"

"I haven't really had time to think about it," said Taylor. "Why?"

"Well," Jenny said, "I'm looking for a project."

"A project?" Jenny didn't seem the project type.

"Yes. I've become really interested in restoring and decorating older buildings. This is a great house, really, if it wasn't so run down. It has good bones. It could be turned into a real showpiece in the right hands."

Taylor wasn't sure whether she should feel complimented or insulted. A little of both maybe.

"You want to buy the house?" She wanted to get this clear.

"Yes. I'm a little bored these days. Kevin is always occupied with business and with the Town Council. You know how it is. And the boys have their own interests. I'm looking for something creative to do with my time. And this house would be perfect."

"What would you do with it once you'd fixed it up?"

"Oh, maybe if I liked it enough, we'd move here. Or if not, I'd sell it."

"I'm sorry, Jenny. I really don't know what I'm going to do with the house yet."

"But, surely, you're not intending to stay in Badger Lake. What on earth would you do here?" Jenny didn't seem to even try to keep the incredulity from her voice.

"The same as I'd do anywhere else. And I didn't say I was staying. I just said I wasn't sure what my plans were yet."

"Well, it would only make sense..."

"Look, Jenny." Taylor interrupted the start of another attack. "I really don't want to talk about it now. I'm tired and hungry, and I just want some time to think. So, if there's nothing more..." Taylor stood. She knew she was being rude, but rudeness seemed to be the only way to deal with Jenny's persistence.

Jenny reluctantly stood up and reached for her purse and keys. "Well, just be sure to call me first when you do decide to sell."

Not if, but when was her wording, Taylor noticed. She remembered Melvin Donovan's assumption she would be staying. Had Aunt Grace confided in him her hopes for Taylor to return? Why did everyone else expect her to be on the next stage out of town?

Well, maybe she'd get some ideas tomorrow. She was meeting Edie for coffee, and surely she'd know what was going on in Badger Lake. That thought was followed by others she'd been setting aside. How did she really feel about Edie and Aunt Grace? Why did she need to feel or think anything? It was none of her business what sort of a relationship they'd had. She decided to just forget it and go on as before, but it was difficult to get out of her mind. *You think you know people, then you get thrown a curve like that.*

Taylor didn't realize the last words had been spoken out loud till she looked into the faces of Tristan and Denver looking up at her expectantly, certain that her words were of benefit to them in some way. *Great!* Now she had started talking to herself.

"Okay, boys. Time for dinner. Then a walk and an early night. I've had my fill of cleaning for today." *Talking to pets is different from talking to yourself, isn't it?*

The knock at the door certainly wasn't welcome to Taylor. She'd had enough company and questions for the day. Again expecting it to be Jack, she opened the door, her mouth open to give him a ready no. She was wrong again. This time, the figure on the doorstep surprised her, as it was a man she didn't recognize.

He wasn't a large man, rather short and wiry with a thin face and deep set blue eyes that seemed slightly familiar. He had large ridges running like parenthesis at the sides of his mouth. He stood still for a moment before saying, "Taylor?" Then, when she failed to give an immediate response, he went on. "You don't look much like your mother. Greg was the one who took after her."

"Who are you? What do you want?" she said shortly, hoping it wasn't an old family friend she'd forgotten, but she was too tired to worry about being rude.

"I guess you wouldn't remember me. It's been a long time. You were only a few years old when I last saw you."

A terrible thought began to form in her mind. In a million years, it couldn't be *him*. But...

"Aren't you going to invite your father in? It's cold out here on the step."

Taylor was too shaken to refuse. She opened the door wordlessly, and he stepped past her, heading straight to the living room. "The old house hasn't changed much in the last twenty or so years," he said, taking a seat on the couch, his eyes continuing to take stock.

"What do you want?" Taylor managed to croak out. She didn't sit down.

"I thought it was about time I reconnected with my only family."

"You want to reconnect after twenty-odd years of not giving a damn? Why in the world would I want to reconnect with a father who deserted his family and hasn't said a bloody word since?" Taylor felt both anger and tears fighting for control, and she didn't want the tears to win.

"You don't know the whole story, Taylor. There were circumstances only your mother and I knew about."

"And you think I'm going to listen to a lot of rationalization and excuses and welcome you back into the fold?"

"I think you're too much your mother's daughter not to give me a fair hearing. Helen may have had her faults, but she was always fair."

Not about to listen to a reference to her mother's faults

from a man who had no right to list them, she stood in front of him, her arms on her hips, hoping to get across with body language what she was struggling to put into words. "I don't want to see you. I don't want to talk to you. I don't care what you do or where you go, but I don't want you here."

"Understandable, I guess," he said, making no move to get up. "Taylor, I know this is a shock, but I need to talk to you, to tell you my side of it. No matter how much you may hate me now, I think you really want and need to know what happened all those years ago."

"I know all I need to know. You walked out on us and never let on where you were or even if you were still alive. My mother was heartbroken."

"Did she say that?"

"She didn't need to. She went into a real tailspin after you left, and that's what led to the accident and what killed her. You killed her."

"That's a little harsh and not accurate," he said, maddeningly calm. "You've had twenty years of Armstrong propaganda to tell you whatever they wanted you to think about me."

"Well, you weren't saying anything to contradict it."

"No," he said, "I wasn't here to tell you my side of it. I'm sorry for that. I should have found a way."

Taylor steeled herself against feeling any sympathy for the sadness in the man's voice. Whatever he felt, he deserved it and more.

"I'm not going to listen to any more," she said. "I want you to go."

He finally stood up. "I expected that's how you'd feel," he said. "But think about it for a while. You might not forgive yourself later if you didn't at least hear me out. I'm staying at the motel on the edge of town. Room 16. I'll be waiting to hear from you."

With that, he walked past her and out the door, leaving Taylor in a daze, wondering if she was imagining what had just happened, or was she in some strange state of fugue brought on by lack of sleep?

She had no intention of contacting him. Her parents had married young and against the wishes of Taylor's grandparents. She knew her father had been a wild one. Marriage to him wasn't what they wanted for their daughter. But her mother had been stubborn, and they had eloped one night.

What had been done couldn't be undone. The Armstrongs had decided to make the best of it. Taylor knew her parents had lived in this house with her grandparents for a while. Eventually, they had moved out into a small house on the edge of town. Her family didn't talk much about what had happened next, but Taylor had heard enough to fill in the blanks. They were young and reckless and spent more than they earned. Her father had worked at the local hardware store. Soon, Greg had been born and a couple of years later, Taylor.

Taylor remembered snatches of conversation from her grandparents about her mother that would end the moment they'd discovered she had been listening. From those snatches, she had known they had begun to quarrel, and her father had not been able to give up his partying lifestyle to stay home and help raise a family. Then, one day, he had just disappeared into thin air, and no one had heard from him since. Her mother had moved with her children back into the family home. Taylor's grandparents had both been in frail health by then, so Aunt Grace had helped mostly with the raising of her and Greg.

Taylor had only a few memories of her mother, and she wasn't sure how many were actual memories and how many were mental pictures drawn by what she'd heard. Greg remembered more, and he used to tell Taylor stories, but maybe he just made them up for her benefit.

She knew her mother had begun to drink heavily and had run around with another "wrong one." Jason Tyler had been too drunk to drive one night and had gone over a steep embankment, rolling the car over and over. Taylor's mother had died. Jason had barely suffered a scratch.

How in the world could her father expect her to forgive him for what had happened to her family? Then she remembered he had never mentioned forgiveness. He'd only asked her to listen. Well, she wasn't going to do that, and he could wither away waiting at the motel as long as he liked while waiting for her to call. She wasn't going to, and that was final.

"Who are you trying to convince, Taylor?" she said. She didn't want to forgive her father, but she would like to know more about her mother. Maybe he could tell her, give her a picture more detailed than the sketchy mind photos she had.

She knew the version of her mother her grandparents gave her was colored by their love and grief. Maybe her father could add another dimension for her. *No!* She wasn't going to call him. Whatever he told her would be for his own interest. She couldn't count on anything he said to be true.

There was one other source she could tap, though. Edie would have been present through all the drama all those years ago. She had been friends with Grace from childhood and would know what had really happened. Or did anyone? She found it strange suddenly that she had never questioned more, wondered more about her father's disappearance and her mother's death. But then, any efforts she did make to question her grandparents had been discouraged or sugar-coated. She supposed she just got used to it and decided to accept the abbreviated version of events as the only one she was going to get. Even Greg hadn't talked about it much.

Taylor sat on the couch, scratching Tristan behind the ears, to his utter joy, as tears of remembrance slowly ran down her cheeks.

Chapter Four

One more step to go. She fought off the vertigo that threatened to consume her. Why was she so frightened? The beam wasn't that small. It was just that it was so high from the ground. She sucked in her breath and took the final step.

The next day, after her breakfast and morning walk were over, Taylor felt at odds. She knew she should start on some more sorting. The stuff in the attic and the contents of the second floor bedrooms needed her attention. She decided to put her father and his visit firmly behind her and not even give him a second thought. It was easier said than done when she had no plans. *No plans?* Of course, she had plans. She was going to fix the house up and sell it. That was her plan. The only reason any other idea, like staying, entered her mind was because she'd used it to put off both Jack and Jenny. Why were they so insistent she sell the house? And sell to them? Was Jack that hard up for a commission or Jenny for a distraction?

She decided to look for a key to the shed. She wanted to see if there was anything worth keeping and maybe find some tools to start working on the yard. She rummaged in kitchen drawers, but didn't find anything. Most people had a junk drawer somewhere. Aunt Grace had several. Then she found a ring with some old keys hanging on a hook beside the fridge. She took them out, and one of them opened the old padlock.

She had to jerk the old door a little to get it open. Even in

the sunlight, the corners were dark. No light fixture anywhere. There was an old lawn mower in the corner. She saw
a few shelves of old containers of weed killer, most of them
probably illegal now, some plant pots, an assortment of
shovels, hoes, and rakes. Grace hadn't done too much garden work this summer. There was even an inhabited cobweb
in one corner. The major part of the room was taken up by a
large, heavy lid resting on the well that used to supply the
house. It seemed strange it had never been filled in, but
maybe her grandparents didn't totally trust the town water
supply and wanted to have a private reserve. Then Aunt
Grace probably put it off so long she forgot about it. In any
case, it would have to be closed off and filled and the shed
torn down and replaced before selling.

She locked the door and, depressed again at the sight of
the garden, went into the house. The best plan was to make
a plan. She grabbed an old steno notebook and pen and
started a list.

Clean stove and fridge—no, make that clean everything.
List items to keep and those for sale.
Clean garden, or better still, hire someone else to do it.
Sort things in attic and in bedrooms.
Call local handyman to see about closing well and tearing
down shed.
Check roof and windows for any problems.

She was pretty sure the roof was okay. There had been a
big hailstorm in Badger Lake a few years ago, and Aunt
Grace's roof, as well as the roofs of nearly every house in
town, was fitted with new shingles.

She checked her watch and realized she only had a few
minutes to clean herself up and get to The Northland to meet
Edie.

Tristan looked at her pleadingly as she went out the door.
"You've already had your walk, and I don't think The Northland would appreciate you as a customer." Tristan knew a
lost cause when he saw one, so he trotted off to annoy the
cat. A dog had to have some fun.

When she walked into the restaurant, it was nearly full.
She saw Jack Vandenberg there, probably chatting up a pro-
spective sale. How much turnover in real estate could there
be in a small town? Jenny was there, too, sitting in a booth
with two other women Taylor didn't recognize. Even Bill and

Evelyn Waters were there. She had to pass their table, and Bill looked as though he was going to say something. Taylor almost swore Evelyn kicked him in the shins under the table. Evelyn gave her a smile, and Taylor couldn't help feeling sorry for her. It had to be difficult being married to a man like Bill Waters.

Feeling a little on display, Taylor sat on a padded bench across from Edie. "Does the whole town come here for coffee?"

"Pretty much. Today is a little busier than usual. I guess I could have suggested somewhere more private to talk. There's Merv's Cafe around the corner from the Co-op. It only gets busy at mealtimes."

"No. This is okay. With this many people talking, no one is going to hear us."

Taylor gave a glance at the table where the Waters were sitting. Bill was looking at her, but shifted his gaze when they made eye contact. "Edie, why is Bill Waters acting so strangely? Did you hear his comment at the funeral? He said something about Aunt Grace being with God, not like Greg. What does he have against Greg?"

Edie spoke in a voice so low Taylor had to strain to hear. "You must remember Rebecca Waters?"

"Oh yes. She was their daughter." Taylor lowered her voice to match Edie's. "I didn't really know her. She was more Greg's age. She went missing, I remember. There was another one, too, from somewhere nearby that disappeared at the same time."

Edie leaned forward. "It's not only too noisy for anyone else to hear, it's too noisy for me to hear, too. Look, come back to the house with me later, and I'll tell you some of the things you may have forgotten or maybe never even knew. You would have been only ten or so at the time."

They went back to their coffee, talking in normal voices about the weather, whether the farmers would get their crops in before frost, and other topics usual to town talk.

"Have you decided what to do about the house?"

"Not yet. I've been trying to list all the things I need to do before selling it. There is so much stuff to sort through. I was even up in the attic yesterday going through old boxes, and I found old books and ornaments and even some old journals of Greg's. I'm not sure what to do with it all."

"You could talk to Jim Bates, the auctioneer, if you want to sell off the furniture and knickknacks. There are always collectors going to country sales, looking for collectibles. I suggest you check everything first to be sure of its value before selling. You may think it's junk, and I might think it's junk, but you never know what people will collect."

"Yes, it's not just Aunt Grace's things. There's a lot of stuff that must go back to my grandparents' time. No one in my family apparently liked to throw things out. That's the trouble with a big house, too much room for storage."

They finished their coffee, and Edie paid the bill over Taylor's protests. She felt eyes on her as they walked out—Jack, Jenny, and the Waters. She swore conversation stopped for a moment. What interest could she possibly hold for them all?

Taylor hadn't been in Edie's house for years. When she came home to visit Aunt Grace, it was usually Edie who stopped in at their house, not the other way around. It was quite a contrast to the big house. A one-story bungalow, it was compact and quite minimal in decor—a modern couch and chair with clean lines, only a couple of side tables and a few ornaments. There were some watercolors on the wall, but no old framed photos or knickknacks. It looked as though it had been freshly painted.

She sat at a square pine table in the kitchen while Edie made coffee, not that they needed more. Homemade oatmeal cookies were set out on the table. Jasper, the golden retriever that once belonged to her aunt, padded into the room to greet her as an old friend.

"How much do you remember about the summer Rebecca went missing?"

"Well," she thought back. "Mostly, I remember how upset Greg was. He was sort of a friend of Rebecca's, or at least went to school with her. I remember they had search parties out looking for her, but I know they never found her."

"Another girl had disappeared a few months earlier."

"I remember that, too. She wasn't from Badger Lake, though."

"No, but it was only about twenty miles away. It turned out there wasn't a connection, because the other girl turned up a few months later in Vancouver. She'd just run off with a boyfriend her parents wouldn't let her see. When he ditched her, she came back home. I think everyone was so relieved we didn't have a serial abductor or killer on the loose, we all forgot that Rebecca never turned up the same way."

"It must be so hard for the Waters, not knowing if she's alive or not."

"Rebecca was their only child, so they had no one to be strong for, and Bill was always a little on the edge. He's never been able to let go, even after all these years."

"It's Evelyn Waters I feel sorry for. She has to put up with Bill and his outbursts. It must get rather embarrassing for her."

"Oh, I think she learned how to cope with Bill a long time ago. She used to be a lot different. She's older than me, but not by a lot. I remember she used to have quite a temper herself. I heard her say once that when she and Bill got married, one of them had to learn how to rein it in, and it obviously wasn't going to be Bill, so she taught herself to be calm, a sort of self-therapy. I always admired her for that."

"So her serenity is just a pose?"

"Oh, I don't think so. Maybe at first, but I think she really changed herself in some fundamental way."

"So what does Bill have against Greg? I remember he was one of the ones out looking for Rebecca when she disappeared."

"Bill and Evelyn were very protective of Rebecca. She was their only child, and, of course, they were a religious family. Rebecca had a lot of restrictions on what she could do and how she was expected to behave. She was expected to go to church, youth group programs, prayer meetings, and all that. Not exactly a young girl's dream life. But she was a quiet girl, dreamy, and quite smart. I don't know where she got her quiet personality from. It must be a recessive gene somewhere."

"But what did all this have to do with Greg?"

"You probably didn't pay too much attention to Greg's friends, but he used to hang around with Jack Vandenberg, Jenny Sandowski, and Tara Leigh Hainsworth."

"Oh, I'd nearly forgotten about Tara Leigh. She used to be a brat, always acting like their leader. I never liked her, and I don't think she thought too much of me either."

"Well, the kids were only twelve or thirteen, but I think Tara Leigh was already setting her sights on Greg. Grace was getting worried about it. Anyhow, Rebecca wasn't part of their group, but she sort of lurked around the edges."

"So, the only reason Bill dislikes Greg is because he was a friend of Tara Leigh's? Or does he think they were leading her astray?"

"A bit of that, maybe. I think Greg liked Rebecca, but I'm not sure the other girls were always kind to her. But mostly, it stems from the day Rebecca went missing."

Taylor tried to picture that day, but all she remembered was confusion and a feeling of fear and dread.

"Greg, Jack, Jenny, and Tara Leigh had all been with Rebecca that day. Heaven knows where they'd been. It was summer holidays. But they were the last ones to see Rebecca, and Bill thought they knew more than they were telling."

"He didn't think they had anything do with her disappearance, did he?" The thought of the overly sensitive Greg harming anyone in any way was ludicrous.

"It wasn't that, exactly. He just thought the kids could have told them more about her last day and about what they were doing. Maybe something she said, or how she felt about things, maybe an argument."

"They were probably listening to music somewhere or pretending to be rock stars or something silly."

"Likely, but that's not how Bill sees it."

"Greg was devastated after Rebecca's disappearance. That's one of the things I do remember. He changed, became more moody. I think maybe that was the start of his problems. I know he was only thirteen, but..."

"We never really know the root of another person's demons. Who even knows what made Bill Waters the way he is?"

"I do think he's crossing the line by suggesting Greg had anything to do with Rebecca's d—" She was going to say death, but changed it. "Disappearance." Why did she feel in her heart that Rebecca was dead?

"I think most people assume now that she's dead." Edie answered her question. "At first, the town just thought she'd gotten tired of the restrictions Bill and Evelyn had set on her and had run off for a bit of freedom. We all expected her to show up one day with a boyfriend or a baby, or maybe both in tow. But, after the years started to pass, everyone was pretty sure she would have contacted someone if she was still alive."

"So what is Badger Lake's verdict? Do they think she committed suicide or had an accident?"

"I think most people think she was depressed and she did something to herself, maybe went into the river."

"But, if so, wouldn't she have been found somewhere?"

"You'd think so, but who knows? It's not something people want to dwell on. When that optometrist committed suicide, we all knew when and why, and it was gossip for months. This is a little different, partly because we don't know and partly because it's a child. No one wants to think anything bad can happen to a child. It's just a little too close to home. So we ignore it and pretend it never happened, and that she's off in California somewhere."

"Well, at least I can understand Bill Waters' behavior a little better. But he can leave Greg out of it. He wouldn't be involved in any way." Then she asked, "Did the police question them? I seem to remember the local police coming to the house back then, but I was shooed away to a friend's house and never heard what it was about."

"Oh yes. The police questioned everyone, adults and kids, but I know they talked to Greg and the other three more than once. Grace was really worried they'd blame them when they couldn't find answers. But, in the end, the searches got called off, the investigation stopped, and everyone began to forget it. Everyone but Bill and Evelyn, of course."

"What do you think happened to Rebecca?"

Edie stopped for a moment to consider. "I think," she began slowly. "I think she's dead. I thought that at the beginning, and I've seen nothing to change my mind. Rebecca wasn't a rebellious child. She may have led a restrictive life and wanted more freedom, but I can't see her going away without any word. She'd have felt guilty hurting anyone."

"But dead how? An accident maybe? Suicide? Running into the wrong person on a late night by herself?"

Edie shrugged. "That, I can't answer. I just feel she's dead."

"What about Bill and Evelyn? Do they feel she's dead, too?"

"Probably. But I'm sure they have flickering hopes. You can't let go of a child completely. I'm sure a part of them expects she'll come home someday. That's what's so sad about not knowing. You face the death of your child every day again and again."

Taylor felt it was time to change the subject. She leaned over and patted Jasper as he laid his head on her knee. "What are you going to do with the kennel? Do you plan to run it as a boarding kennel again?"

"I'm not sure yet. I'd like to keep it going. It was never very busy, just a few dogs at any given time, but there is a market for one in Badger Lake, and it would be nice to have something to do."

"I'm sorry, Edie. You must miss her terribly."

Edie sighed and stood up to refill the coffee cups. "What do they say? Life must go on. We had a long time together, and I'm thankful for that." Edie's eyes went to the dog. "What about Jasper? Would you like to keep him? I took him in when Grace had to go to the hospital, but he's yours really."

"Oh no. I've already got one dog and one cat, and they're enough to keep me busy. If you want Jasper, he's all yours. He's a lovely dog, but more than I can handle with the others."

She thought Edie let out a long breath after that statement. She had obviously wanted Jasper, but felt compelled to ask Taylor first.

"I'd better get home and look after my two. Thanks for the coffee, Edie, and the cookies." She suddenly didn't feel like a conversation about her father. It could wait till another day.

Tristan and Denver both gave her the once-over when she got back. She wondered if Tristan recognized Jasper's scent. They used to play together. She always brought Tristan when she came to visit, but left Denver at home with her neighbor as carer. Cats weren't as fond of traveling as dogs.

She had a late lunch, fortified till then by the oatmeal cookies and coffee, then decided she'd better take another stab at the cleaning. She vacuumed and dusted the downstairs rooms and then cleaned out the fridge, leaving it to defrost. When she was dusty and tired, she took Tristan for a walk and then fired up her laptop. It was time to get some of her own work done. It took most of the afternoon just to catch up on her e-mail and networking. By then, she had no desire to work and her creativity bug had left her.

She turned on the television and began to watch a soap opera she hadn't seen in years. Feeling a little guilty, she pulled the curtains closed, then scolded herself. If she wanted to watch a soap opera in the afternoon, it was nobody's business but hers. She soon turned it off anyhow. She only recognized a few of the characters and even they were being portrayed by new actors.

Instead, she went upstairs and climbed into the attic again, this time armed with a flashlight. It still didn't shed much light. Maybe she should get a stronger bulb, but she didn't feel like climbing back down again. She rooted in the box where she had seen Greg's journals and brought them downstairs. She wasn't sure if she should read them or not. It seemed an invasion to read someone else's private thoughts, but she wondered if maybe they would give her a clue to the turns Greg's life had taken.

She opened the first one. It was dated July 2nd, the year Greg had been ten and Taylor had just turned eight.

Went to watch the Canada Day parade yesterday, and Aunt Grace let us stay for the fireworks. They were awesome! Taylor was scared of the fireworks. She is such a baby! Jack and Jenny stayed, too, and we were able to hang out. Tara Leigh had a cold, and her mom made her stay home. She was mad. When we got home, Aunt Grace let us stay up and have cake and ice cream. I had ice cream three times yesterday.

Taylor thumbed through the next few pages, and they were more of the same. Not very explicit or informative. Just comments on how they spent the day. The four of them were inseparable even then. Nearly every day, they were doing something together, but Taylor saw nothing there that could indicate the problems that came later.

She rummaged in the pile and found a later one. It started in May, just before the summer of the year Rebecca went missing.

She flicked into it and was stopped by a mention of Rebecca's name.

I don't know why Tara Leigh hates Rebecca so much. She's a really nice kid if she would only give her a chance. She's terribly smart, too, but you can't always tell because she's so shy. Tara Leigh got cross yesterday because I sat with Rebecca at lunch time. When the rest of them got to the table, Tara Leigh started making mean comments about Rebecca's dad and how crazy he was about religion. When I stuck up for her and told Tara Leigh to cool it, she yelled at me and stormed off. She never spoke to me again until after school. Jack says she's jealous, but that's just stupid.

A few pages farther on:

Tara Leigh is acting a lot better now toward Rebecca. She even asked her to sit with us at lunch today. She told her maybe she could even come with us sometimes when we go to the old creamery. That's our special place, so that says a lot about how Tara Leigh is trying to be better. I'm glad because I like both of them, and it's no fun when your friends hate each other.

Taylor set the journal aside and put the lot of them in a box she'd started to fill with ornaments. She would try to get back to them tomorrow, but now it was time to take care of supper. Denver had begun to wrap himself around her ankles, and Tristan was making snuffling noises as he did when he was getting hungry.

It would be an early bedtime tonight. She was strangely tired, and she hadn't really done that much. Maybe it was aftershock. It was only the day before yesterday they had buried Aunt Grace, but it seemed eons ago.

She lay in bed, feeling terribly tired but not able to sleep. She finally gave up and turned on the light, pulling an old Agatha Christie from the bookshelf—Aunt Grace's favorite author. She'd read them all, but maybe that's what she needed to lull herself to sleep, something familiar. It worked. Twenty minutes later, she turned out the light and drifted off.

She awoke in the dark to a low growling coming from Tristan. Then he gave a couple of short woofs and grabbed the covers, pulling them from the bed. Taylor sat up quickly. She heard someone moving in the house. It was coming from the attic. Tristan was now scratching at the door to get out.

"No way," Taylor whispered. "Whoever's there is probably bigger than me and certainly bigger than you. Sh. Be quiet."

Her cell phone was charging on the bedside table. Thank heavens she hadn't left it downstairs. She dialed 9-1-1 and then realized Badger Lake wasn't set up for the 9-1-1 service. She didn't know the police number by heart, and probably no one would be there in the night anyhow. The only number she knew was Edie's. She hated to wake her and alarm her, but she wasn't about to leave this room. She dialed. Edie's voice answered, surprisingly awake.

She whispered as loudly as she dared "Edie, can you call the police? There's someone in the house. I think they're in the attic."

"Hang up."

She did, and it was only minutes later that she saw lights flashing through her window—car lights. No siren, but whoever was upstairs knew it was time to leave. She heard a clatter in the hallway from someone half-falling down the ladder and footsteps racing downstairs. The lights flashed again and disappeared.

About ten minutes later, there was a knock on the door and a loud voice said, "Taylor? It's Sergeant Scott. I'm coming in. The door's open."

By now, she had managed to climb into some jeans and a sweatshirt. She met him at the bottom of the stairs.

"You didn't leave your door unlocked?"

"No, of course not. I always lock up."

He looked down at her from his considerable height advantage and said in a skeptical tone, "There's no sign of a break-in. The door is quite intact."

"That may be, but I locked the door. Someone must have broken in somehow." No six-foot-plus cop in cowboy boots and jeans was going to intimidate her. Then she gave a guilty start.

"Yes?" he prompted.

"Aunt Grace used to leave a spare key hidden outside in case she was ever locked out, and I just left it there."

"Let me guess," he said. "Under a flower pot?" He nudged a container of desiccated begonia blooms with his toe, and a key on a red ring appeared. "I imagine there are probably about two people in Badger Lake that don't know where she hides the key." Then he smiled, and she forgave him for the slights on her security breach. His smile had the melting power of a warm Calgary Chinook. Now where did that come from? Taylor was not normally prone to flights of fancy.

She remembered her manners. No matter what time of day or night, Aunt Grace would never leave someone on the doorstep without an offer of nourishment. "Would you like a cup of coffee?"

"I'd love one, but I think, right now, we both need sleep. I do need to get some details from you for my report. If I come by tomorrow morning around ten, will you still offer me coffee?"

"I might even find a cookie to go with it."

"I'll just take a quick look to be sure everything is all right. I tried to follow the guy around the back, but, with not much in the way of streetlights, he slipped off into the dark." The sergeant disappeared up the stairs followed by Tristan, and she heard him pulling the ladder up again. Back downstairs, he handed her the key, and said, "Best keep this inside now." And he backed out of the driveway with a little flutter of gravel.

Taylor started up the stairs again, then remembered Edie. Should she call her to say everything was okay? She would probably just wake her up again. She opened the door to Greg's old room and looked out toward the direction of Edie's house. She remembered when the back lane was edged on two sides by tall stands of trees, but now they had been thinned and cropped, and she could just make out the outlines of two houses. She thought she could tell which one was Edie's, and there was a small light on upstairs. She'd take a chance and call.

She was right. Edie answered on the first ring.

"Everything okay now?"

"Yes, Sergeant Scott checked around. He didn't catch whoever it was, but the house is all locked up now, the spare key is no longer there, and I can't see anyone coming back."

"Did Andrew give you his number just in case?"

"Andrew?"

"Sergeant Scott."

"Oh. No, he didn't."

"Well, here is his home number. Write it down and put it beside your bed just in case."

Chapter Five

One shaky foot in front of the other along the beam. She held her arms outstretched just as Jenny had done, balancing herself. She willed herself not to look down. Look ahead, straight ahead. Look at the wall. Now move one more foot. It will soon be over.

Sergeant Andrew Scott looked a little different when he came at ten the next morning. Instead of jeans and a tank top under an open windbreaker, he was now official-looking with the striped blue trousers, the gray shirt, and clunky boots. He looked a lot bigger and much more formidable. The comfortable feeling of last night was gone. He dropped his hat on the table and sat down at her invitation.

"Cream and sugar?" she asked as she poured the coffee into the only two matching mugs she could find in the cupboard. Aunt Grace's cupboards were full of matching china tea sets, but, when it came to mugs, she had a one-off style, most of them souvenirs with inscriptions on them.

"Just one sugar." He stirred his coffee and took a tentative sip before setting his mug back down. "Have you had a chance to look around and see if anything's missing?"

"It's the strangest thing," Taylor said. She remembered last night's promise of a cookie with his coffee and set a plate on the table of some chocolate marshmallow ones she had found in a cupboard. Hopefully, they hadn't gone stale. She went on. "It seems the only place he looked was the attic. There's nothing of value there. I had my laptop downstairs, the television, an e-reader, and a tablet, the things you'd think someone would steal, but they're all here. What could he be looking for in the attic?"

"You're sure nothing is gone?" Andrew bit into the cookie and finished it with two bites, reaching for a second. Apparently, they weren't stale. Either that or he hadn't had time for breakfast.

"I couldn't be positive, because there are boxes and boxes of junk up there, and I haven't looked into most of them. Some of it goes back to my grandparents. But I can't see anything obviously gone."

"Well, I'm sorry to say, but it looks like a write-off. I don't imagine we'll find him unless he does something like it again." He cast a glance at the cookie plate, but must have decided on a two-cookie limit as he lifted his coffee mug instead.

"So he didn't conveniently catch his pants on a shrub, or drop a bracelet, or something to leave a clue?"

"In real life, it seldom works out that way." He smiled and finished his coffee. "I'm sorry you were frightened, but I bet he got a pretty fair scare, too. He's not likely to come back." He stood and fingered his cap. "Are you planning on staying in Badger Lake?"

"I'm not sure what my plans are, but you're about the fourth person in the last couple of days to ask me that question. Everyone seems to have a strange interest in my plans."

"Really? Oh well, you know what small towns are like."

"I'd forgotten, but it's all coming back." She hesitated, then plunged in, realizing she was about to do the same thing she had accused the town of doing. "Can I ask you something totally off the subject?"

"My favorite kind of question."

"What do you know about the disappearance of Rebecca Waters?"

He sucked in his breath and sat down again. "It's before my time, I'm afraid. I've heard a lot of talk about it, but I don't know anything more than anyone else in town."

"Aren't there records at the station?"

"Probably, if I were to look, although they might not be on the computers. What brought on this interest in Rebecca Waters?"

"She used to hang out sometimes with my brother, Greg,

and his friends." She was going to stop there, but suddenly decided to press on and tell him about Bill Waters' strange behavior and cryptic words. "I've just been trying to figure out why he thought Greg would know anything about her disappearance or death."

"I wouldn't put too much stock in anything Bill Waters says. He has a tendency to go off on a rant, and, at one time or another, he's had a go at nearly everyone in town. People usually just try to ignore him."

"I guess I'll have to do the same," said Taylor. "It's his wife Evelyn I feel sorry for, having to put up with him on a daily basis."

He stood up again. "Well, let me know if you have any more problems". He scribbled a number on the back of a card and set it on the table. "That's my cell phone and home numbers if you have any more nighttime visitors." Taylor didn't bother telling him she already had them.

Taylor wanted another look at the attic. Was there something there she was missing? Something of value? But, if there was, it had been there for years. Taylor was pretty sure nothing new had been added to the junk up there lately. Aunt Grace had been in no shape to climb, and, if she had wanted something added to or taken from the attic, she would have asked Taylor on one of her visits to do it for her.

She pulled down the ladder, taking with her the stronger-watt bulb she had commandeered from a hallway. She made a mental note to add light bulbs to her next grocery list. It showed things a little more clearly, but still gave no clue as to what someone would want to steal. Some boxes had been disturbed and books thrown around, but that was all she could make out. She restored order to the book boxes and went back downstairs.

She grabbed Tristan's leash and headed out on her now familiar route. Tristan was taking to Badger Lake quite nicely. He had already made friends with a black lab and a shepherd cross and, for some reason, taken a dislike to a small white dog of mixed heritage. On the way back, she passed the kennel and saw the front door open a crack and the light on.

She walked in to the office area where Aunt Grace had also kept kibble and other pet staples for sale as a sideline. Edie was there, tidying up the area and commenting as she did to a boxer dog who sat beside her, head cocked to one side, listening to her every word.

"Good conversationalist, is he?" Taylor asked.

Edie turned. "You're not supposed to sneak up on old women. We might die of fright."

Taylor snorted. "Whatever you die of, Edie, it's not going to be of fright. Who's your friend?"

By now, the boxer and Tristan had exchanged their version of an introduction and seemed to have a mutually favorable opinion of each other.

"Well, I guess I've sort of decided to go ahead with the kennel," Edie said. "I just got my first customer. I didn't think anyone even knew we were still here."

"Someone holidaying at the lake?"

"Not really. You'd never guess who it is."

"Who?"

"Tara Leigh Bridgeman, as she's called now."

"What in the world is she doing back in Badger Lake?"

"Visiting her old friend, Jenny, apparently. One of Jenny's kids is allergic to dogs, so Tara Leigh dropped her boxer off here last night."

"Tara Leigh and Jenny used to be good friends, but they can't see much of one another if Tara Leigh didn't even know Jenny's kids had allergy problems."

"She didn't seem too happy about it. I guess I'd better check and make sure I still have an up-to-date business license to take in boarders. I wonder what else I'll have to do. A lot of tidying up, I know."

"So you've decided to go ahead?"

"For now anyhow, maybe just taking in the odd dog. I don't really care about making it a thriving business or anything, but I do like to look after dogs." She stopped to scratch the boxer on the side of his ear. "His name is Felix."

"Felix? That's a cat's name." Changing the subject, she asked, "How long is Tara Leigh going to be in town?"

"She said just a few days."

"I wonder if she'll try to buy the house and ask me how long I'm staying, too."

"Pardon?"

"Well, Jack is following me around town trying to buy the house. Jenny came over to see me about it. She told me she wants a 'project.' Maybe they're recruiting help to convince me to put the house up for sale. Tara Leigh's the only one of Greg's old group that hasn't been harassing me."

"I can't see Jenny as a project kind of person. She must be bored. I know Kevin seems to have other interests these days, so maybe she needs to fill in time."

"How can she be bored? She has kids. Keeping up with kids and their sports and activities is pretty much a full-time job these days. Jenny was always the athletic type. If she's bored, you'd think she'd be off coaching soccer teams or something."

"She used to be really into gymnastics, I remember. Too bad, in a small town like Badger Lake, there's not too much prospect for developing kids' athletic skills. Unless it's hockey, of course."

"Hmm. Well, I'd better get back to my tidying, too. Honestly, there's so much stuff to go through, I don't know where to start. In addition to everything in the attic, there are boxes of papers and letters in Aunt Grace's closet, and I don't know what needs to be kept. If I get caught up, I'll come and give you a hand."

"I'm fine. There's not that much to do here. You've got your hands full enough."

Taylor dropped Tristan off to keep Denver company and decided to take a trip to the post office to see if any mail had caught up with her. It had, but not the kind she was interested in. As she was leaving, she met Evelyn Waters starting up the steps, by herself, thank heavens.

"I hear you had a break-in last night."

Taylor smiled. "I knew it wouldn't take long for word to circulate. I don't suppose the town grapevine has decided yet who the intruder was?"

"I'm sure everyone has their own ideas. Did they manage to get away with anything?"

"No, I didn't see anything missing. The strange thing is he was up in the attic, and there's nothing of value there, so I don't know what he was looking for."

Evelyn had turned to go into the post office and stumbled, catching her heel on a step. She reached out and grabbed Taylor's arm to steady herself. "Sorry about that. I sprained my ankle a while ago, and every once in a while, it does something like that."

"Are you sure you're all right? You look a little shaken."

"I'm fine. It's just, at my age, you don't want to take a fall. It's a little scary when you stumble."

Taylor watched as she stepped inside, thinking that Evelyn was much less frail than she sounded. Her hold on Taylor's arm was like a vise grip. She wouldn't be surprised to see bruises there tomorrow.

The police cruiser passed by on the street and Andrew gave her a cheery wave. Policing was a lot different in a small town, she thought. She wondered what it would be like to have to arrest someone you knew, perhaps had had coffee with. But then, what crime could there be in a town like Badger Lake?

Taylor attacked her cleaning with a half-hearted effort. Then, tired of the physical labor, she decided to have another go at Greg's journals. Maybe they would tell her more about Rebecca and her relationship with Greg and his friends—The Famous Four. She selected one at random and began to read.

Tara Leigh is at it again. I thought she'd decided to be nice to Rebecca, but today, when Rebecca and I were working on an English assignment together, Tara Leigh sat down beside us and began making snarky comments. Then she knocked over a bottle of Coke onto all of Rebecca's notes. She apologized and said it was an accident, but I think she did it on purpose. The Coke splashed all down the front of Rebecca's shirt, too. She jumped up and ran off. I wish Tara Leigh wasn't so mean, and I wish Rebecca would learn to fight back or at least ignore her. It's not much fun when two people you like don't like each other.

Poor Greg. He was always the peacemaker, Taylor remembered, the one who could always see both sides of a story. Personally, Taylor had rather liked Rebecca, although she thought she was a little bit of a rabbit. Rebecca had helped her once with her homework when she'd come by the house while Greg was out. Tara Leigh, on the other hand, she had never liked. Her mind began to wander from the journals. She wondered what prompted Tara Leigh to come back to Badger Lake all of a sudden. People were not acting at all as they should have been acting, and that bothered Taylor. It was when Greg's behavior started changing that his troubles began.

Still no insight into Rebecca's disappearance. A spilled Coke and disagreements with a friend didn't add anything to solving the puzzle. She should have read some more, but her eyes were tired, and she was ready for bed. Last night's interrupted sleep had caught up to her. She realized she hadn't called yet to have someone change the locks. That would have to wait until tomorrow.

Chapter Six

She stopped after three steps, feeling the beam shivering, or was that her? Below, she heard one of them suck in their breath. She wondered if it was Greg. If he wasn't watching, she knew she'd take the two steps back and run down the ladder and home. They could all take a flying leap, all except Greg. Other than that, it was silent. She moved her left foot ahead. It caught on something, the edge of a knothole.

Taylor woke wondering if she had dreamed her visitor last night. She was trying to decide whether to tackle Edie and pursue the matter or just forget it had happened.

Her phone rang as she poured her first coffee of the day. "Taylor? It's Edie. Have you heard the news?"

"No. What's happened?"

"It's Tara Leigh. She's dead."

"Tara Leigh? She can't be. She just got here." It hit her that there was no logic to that statement, but sudden death had that effect on her. "How? She's too young for a heart attack."

"Her car went into the river down by the bend on that old road south of the lake. The tow truck pulled the car out. She was in it, alone, thank heavens."

"What was she doing out there? And alone?"

"Who knows? Maybe she was visiting old haunts and wanted to be alone. Maybe she lost control. I'm sure she's not used to driving on gravel roads now, especially at night."

"Why don't you come over for coffee, Edie? I just made fresh."

"I can't right now. I have to go look after Felix, and Jasper hasn't had his morning walk yet. I just got up when the phone rang. It was Ethel Summers with the news. She lives out by the lake and saw the police car and tow truck. I imagine she's phoned nearly everyone in Badger Lake by now. Why don't you meet me for coffee at The Northland at ten?"

"Okay. Half the town will be there at ten o'clock, I bet."

"Probably more than half this morning. It will be the number one topic of conversation."

Taylor hung up. At least they'd probably find out more over coffee. *Oh great!* Now she was becoming just like the rest of the town, anxious to get the dirt on everyone and having gossip sessions over coffee. She sighed. *You can take the girl out of the small town*, she paraphrased.

If Edie hadn't already been there and secured a table in the far corner, Taylor would have had no place to sit at The Northland. She walked by a table with Evelyn and Bill Waters, another where Jack Vandenberg sat with three other men, and others filled with people she recognized by sight but couldn't put a name to. Notably missing was Jenny. That was only natural, but she thought one of the men sitting with Jack was probably Kevin, Jenny's husband.

She slid into the seat across from Edie. "Is this a wake?" Taylor asked.

"Actually, it's not much different from any morning. Ten o'clock is always coffee time in Badger Lake. Anyone who isn't here is over in Merv's Cafe. Most of the local farmers meet there."

"Have you heard anything new?"

"Not really. No one knows anything other than what Ethel saw out by the lake. Jenny's husband, Kevin, said Tara Leigh got a phone call and said she was going out for a bit. She never told them who called or why."

"Maybe it was her family calling and she had bad news. That would have affected her driving," Taylor said.

"I imagine her husband would have called on her cell. This call came on the house phone, apparently. And if her family had called, it wasn't something that would have sent her out by the lake."

"That means it was someone local. I imagine the town

will find out eventually who it was and what, if anything, it had to do with her heading out for the lake. Has anyone heard from Andrew?"

"He'll be too busy now, and, of course, he won't be able to talk about it. Josie, on the other hand, has been known to let the odd thing slip out."

"Josie?"

"She's the dispatcher, secretary, filer, whatever, at the police station. She's Norman Cross's daughter."

"Oh right, she went to school here, but she was behind me a year or two. Has anyone been in touch with Tara Leigh's family?"

"I'm sure Andrew has contacted her husband. That must be one of the difficult parts of being a policeman."

A tall man with a thin face dressed in coveralls stood in the doorway a moment before heading for a booth with a single occupant.

"That's Gus from the garage. It would be his tow truck that pulled her out."

Suddenly, Taylor began to feel like a vulture, waiting for the meaty bits to come out so they could feed on them. "I have to get out of here, Edie. I don't really feel like coffee anymore."

Edie sensed what she was feeling. "We're not insensitive, you know. The hunger for details isn't because we love to wallow in other people's misfortunes."

"Misfortunes? She's dead!"

"And everyone here is sorry about that. Wanting to know is just a way of expressing concern, it's not voyeurism. This is just how small towns act."

"Then why do I feel like a voyeur?"

"Probably because you knew her, and because we were talking about her yesterday, and because we both said un-kind things about her."

"Let's just talk about something else."

"All right. How are you coming with your renovation plans?"

"Not doing very well. I keep getting sidetracked. I guess I'd better get calling people today. I want someone to come and look at that old shed to see about pulling it down and filling in the well. The place needs a good paint job, but I can do that myself. Then I need to talk to the auctioneer about a date for a sale."

"So you're not planning to stay in Badger Lake?"

"It was never in my plans. I have a life back home, an apartment, friends..." Taylor trailed off. Her best friend had just moved across the country, and the closest thing she had to a boyfriend had recently gone looking for greener pastures. Maybe that's why she felt so ambivalent about the house. *Ambivalent?* Of course, she wasn't ambivalent. She was going to sell and go back home. The end.

She looked up to see Edie grinning at her. "Take some time to make your mind up," she said. "You don't have anything pressing to get back to?"

"No, since my work follows me, I'm really a free agent. And, of course, Denver and Tristan are here, seemingly happy about their new digs."

"Then just tackle things one at a time and see how you feel when the house is ready for sale."

"You're thinking I should stay in Badger Lake?"

"I'm not thinking anything. Just don't rush into decisions. And that's words of wisdom coming from someone with years of experience."

"Edie, there's something I want to ask you," she began.

She saw Edie's glance slide up over her shoulder and turned to see Jack standing there.

"Quite a shocker about Tara Leigh, isn't it?"

"Quite." Taylor didn't really want to continue the conversation, but Jack's coffee buddies had left, and she felt compelled to ask him to sit.

He did with no further prompting. "It's been ages since she's been back in town. We didn't really know her anymore."

"Oh, I thought she and Jenny had kept up their friendship. Wasn't it Jenny she came to see?"

"I guess so. She was staying at Jenny's. But I think she came to see some cousins about some farmland outside town that Tara Leigh and her husband still had a share in. I think Jenny was convenient for her, better than staying in a hotel anyhow."

Jack seemed to be deliberately distancing both himself and Jenny from Tara Leigh. Why?

"Well, I'd better be off." Jack stood and added, "Don't forget, I'm willing to take that house off your hands as-is, no worry on your part about fixing it up."

"I'm considering all angles, Jack. I'll let you know."

They finished their coffee and walked home, neither one talking, both probably thinking much the same things.

When they got to Taylor's drive, Edie said, "What were you going to ask me before Jack came along?"

"Nothing important." Taylor didn't feel up to an emotionally charged conversation about her parents right now. It could wait. She smiled at Edie, then turned and walked toward the door.

Tristan, as usual, was begging for a walk when she opened the door. She obliged him and, on the way home, saw the police car sitting in front of the kennel. She knew she shouldn't have, but curiosity got the better of her, and she stopped to see what Andrew had to say.

He was just finishing the conversation, or at least finished it when she arrived. He gave her a grin and said, "No more break-ins, I hope."

"No, it was quiet last night. I guess you scared him away."

"Probably realized you had nothing he wanted. No reports of break-ins anywhere else in town, so maybe it was a one-time thing. We'll hope so. Badger Lake is usually pretty law-abiding. Doesn't give my detective skills much of a workout."

Taylor looked inquiringly at Edie after he left. "Anything new?"

"Mostly, he wanted to know what frame of mind Tara Leigh was in when she dropped Felix off."

"So, does he think there's a possibility her death was deliberate? I can't believe that, not the Tara Leigh I remember. She would never commit suicide."

"That was a few years ago, Taylor. People change, and you never really know another person."

Too right. Taylor thought again about the long-term relationship between Aunt Grace and Edie that she'd never suspected for a moment.

"He did ask me one strange question." Edie looked thoughtful.

"What? Don't keep me in suspense."

"He asked if I smelled alcohol on her breath when she dropped off Felix."

"And did you?"

"No."

"Once, when we were young—it would have been around

the time Rebecca disappeared, Greg and Tara Leigh would have been around thirteen—Tara Leigh brought over a bottle of vodka, and she and Greg finished the bottle out in the backyard by the shed. Of course, maybe it wasn't full to begin with. I found it the next morning by the back step and hid it so Aunt Grace wouldn't see it. Maybe Tara Leigh had a problem even then. I mean, look at what happened to Greg. It's funny. That was one time the other two weren't with them. It might mean something."

"You needn't have hidden the bottle. Grace knew about it. She told me the next day but thought it would be best not to say anything. As far as I know, it never happened again, at least, not until they were a little older."

"Isn't it funny the things kids think they can hide from their parents and rarely do?"

"Almost as funny as the things the parents do that the kids are unaware of."

"I guess kids just never think of adults having a life outside of them, while parents are sure the kids are only doing the things they did when they were young." She gave Edie a long look. "I'm glad you and Aunt Grace had each other. I really am." Then she gave Edie a quick hug. "Well, I'm off to look after my 'kids.' Let me know if you need any help with Felix or any other boarders you get."

"I wonder what's going to happen to Felix now. I imagine Tara Leigh's husband will be coming for him. You know, it's strange. I don't even know if they have any children. Well, see you tomorrow. You did get those locks changed, didn't you?"

"Oops. I was going to call this morning and forgot with everything else that was happening. I'll go see someone now. I don't imagine it makes any difference. Whoever he was didn't take the key. He put it back when he was done with it."

Taylor took Tristan home, checked on Denver, and spent an hour answering e-mails and texts and taking care of her other social media obligations. Then she walked downtown to the repair shop on Beecher Street, just off Main, to talk to Jimmy. He was the local handyman who did a little of everything besides running a repair shop.

The repair shop looked as if it had been around as long as Badger Lake. It had old wood floors sloping slightly away from the walls and a couple of cracked window panes. The counter at the front by the door had a glass top holding a cash register that might have been around since the beginning of time. The room was full of old appliances, bits of furniture, and a good many items Taylor was hard pressed to identify.

When Taylor told him what she wanted, Jimmy agreed to install new locks on her doors. He was a thin, wiry man with a slight stoop in his stance probably from leaning over his repair table for so many years, and he spoke with a slight burr that suggested his origins were in Scotland. "Heard about your break-in," he said. "They get away with anything?"

"Doesn't look like it. I guess Sergeant Scott arrived in time to scare him away. He suggested I should get new locks with a dead-bolt."

"Aye, Andrew's a good lad. He's from around here originally. His family farmed about ten miles north of Badger Lake. Think they're all dead or moved now, though."

"Oh, I thought they never posted men to their home areas, something to do with having friends they might have to arrest," said Taylor, not sure where she had picked up that tidbit.

"Don't know. Andrew lived away for years before he was sent here, so maybe they figured he didn't have any close friends still around. Anyhow, not much chance of having to arrest a friend in Badger Lake. We're pretty law-abiding here."

"Except for my intruder."

"Yep, except for your intruder." Jimmy looked at her as if it might be her fault the law-abiding reputation of Badger Lake just got a blemish.

"I had some other things I'd like you to look at when you have time," said Taylor. "I want to do something about that old shed in the backyard, and there are a couple of windows that might need replacing upstairs. There's quite a draft coming in."

"I'll be around sometime tomorrow at lunchtime to do the locks. I can look at the other things then and give you an estimate."

Surprised at how quickly he was going to do the work, Taylor hastily said, "I'll be home at lunch tomorrow."

She stopped off at the post office on the way home and again ran into Evelyn Waters. She had been standing in the vestibule and came out just as Taylor started up the steps.

"Anything more on your prowler?" she asked.

"No, there probably won't be if he doesn't try it again somewhere. Maybe it wasn't even someone from around here, could have been a passerby."

"Hmm. You said he didn't take anything? That seems strange. Where was he looking?"

"The only place he seemed to be interested in was the attic, and there's nothing of value there, just old books and diaries and broken furniture." It seemed uncharacteristic of Evelyn to be asking for information. Taylor had never had her pinned down as one of the town's gossips. Maybe she was just lonely. Heaven knew she had a lot to cope with in her life. She thought she had hit on a good assumption when she heard Evelyn's next question.

"Maybe some afternoon I can stop by for coffee?" asked Evelyn. "I'd really like to talk to you, since you were one of my daughter's friends."

"Actually, it was my brother, Greg, who was Rebecca's friend. I hardly knew her."

"Still, I remember her talking about you."

Taylor didn't know how to respond. On the one hand, she wanted to be kind to Evelyn, but she didn't want to start a pseudo-friendship that could be difficult to keep in line. Lonely people could make difficult relationships. "Sure, we'll get together some day, but right now I have a lot to do, straightening up the place to get it ready to sell."

"You're aren't staying then?"

"Selling has always been my intention."

"I thought I heard something about you staying on in Badger Lake. I think it was Jack Vandenberg that said that."

"Well, I haven't exactly made Jack my confidant, so he doesn't know any more about my plans than the rest of the town." She thought she sounded a bit waspish, but she was getting tired of the whole town considering whether she was going to stay or not.

She turned to go into the post office, but Evelyn wasn't quite through. "I did want to tell you not to pay much attention to the things Bill says. He gets funny ideas in his head sometimes."

"Understood. I'll not take offense, I promise." She turned with finality to show the conversation was over, but when she stopped at the row of boxes to check her—well, Aunt Grace's—mailbox, she saw Evelyn still standing there watching her. Why did she feel that Evelyn had staged the encounter in the first place? Maybe she had to do a lot of that, married to Bill. She must spend a lot of time trying to make up for his outbursts and apologizing.

Taylor buckled down to a good sorting in the attic. She filled big garbage bags with old books that weren't really readable now in style or in condition. Some had huge watermarks on them. Then she picked out some that might find a home in the hospital or care home. One or two she remembered as being hers or Greg's, and out of nostalgia, she marked them for keeping. There were some Judy Blume books as well as nearly a whole set of the original Nancy Drews. Those, along with some westerns that probably belonged to her grandfather, some romances, and pioneer stories were set aside for an auction sale. That was her next chore—to talk to the auctioneer and pick a date for a sale. He was probably booked up with farm and estate sales, but he'd likely be able to slip in a small one. Maybe, if she didn't have too much, he could add them to a bigger sale on consignment.

She didn't see anything belonging to her mother stored in the attic and wondered whatever happened to her personal items. Then she wondered if any remnant of her father's life was left in this house. She didn't want to go there in her thoughts. It wasn't likely anyhow. He hadn't lived here long, and, if he had left anything behind, it wouldn't rank as a keepsake to her grandparents.

Just as she was slipping the ladder into its rightful slot, she heard a knock at the door. She was surprised to see Andrew Scott standing there. He wasn't in uniform either. It was amazing what a difference it made. He seemed less imposing and much better looking.

"Your coffee was so good the other day I thought I'd see if I could get a refill." He grinned. "Sorry, bad joke," he said, probably in response to her expression. "I came for two reasons."

"Well you'd better come in and tell me about them. The coffee is a given. I was just going to make some. I don't have cobwebs in my hair, do I?"

"No, why?"

She didn't want to say she thought he was looking at her strangely. "I was just up in the attic going through a bunch of things. It's a bit primitive up there."

"You look great," he said with conviction.

"What did you want to see me about?" She poured the water into the coffee maker and sorted through the cupboard for something to go with it. She found a box of toasted coconut cookies. She hadn't seen those in ages, but they were a favorite when they were kids.

"First was just a follow up to be sure you changed your locks."

"I talked to Jimmy today, and he's coming over at noon tomorrow to take care of it. What was the other thing?"

"Did Tara Leigh contact you at all?"

"No. Why on earth would she? We were never friends. I thought she came to visit Jenny."

"Apparently, she did, but I talked to her husband on the phone, and he seemed to think she was coming to see you."

He took the coffee she offered in a Charles and Diana mug and added two spoons of sugar and a good helping of half and half. He stirred the cup counter-clockwise. Taylor had never seen anyone stir coffee that way before. She wondered if he was left-handed or if it was just an idiosyncrasy.

"She told him that?"

"I think her words were 'I have to talk to Greg's little sister, what's her name.'"

"Well, she never tried, unless she called when I was out. Is it important in some way? I thought it was an accident, her driving into the lake, I mean."

"As far as I know, it was. I just wanted to follow up on anything she did that day."

"Was she drinking?"

"Good old Badger Lake coffee gossip?"

"It wasn't gossip. You asked Edie if she smelled alcohol on Tara Leigh. Well, I guess it was gossip."

"Well, everyone will know, so yes, she did have an empty bottle in the front seat of the car. The coroner's report isn't in, so we don't know her alcohol level yet."

"Is there going to be an inquest?"

"That's up to the coroner. He decides whether the death needs to be investigated further and, if so, whether there will be an inquest. He'll schedule the autopsy."

"They have to do an autopsy?"

"If there's no known underlying cause of death, yes. Then the coroner goes over the medical report and any other information he has and decides if we need to continue to investigate."

"Will her husband be coming to Badger Lake?"

"That's why they're having the autopsy right away. He's getting into town tonight."

"Poor man. It must be quite a shock. Do you know if they have kids?"

"Not so far as I know."

"So what will the coroner say?"

He grinned. "Now you're asking me to be a fortune teller?"

"No, but I imagine you have a good idea."

"Well, unless some new evidence comes up, I imagine it will be ruled an accident. I'm sure the alcohol level will be mentioned. Any more questions?"

"What made you come back to Badger Lake? Someone said you were from around here originally."

"You do jump around all over the place with your questions, don't you?" He put down his coffee and settled in the chair as though he were getting comfortable to watch a movie. Lacing his fingers together over his belt, he started, "Well, my parents farmed over by Greenway. I went to elementary school there, but we moved when I was a teenager. You get to make requests for postings—no guarantee you'll get it— but I remembered Badger Lake as a nice place, so here I am."

"Oh. You must know most of the people here."

"I've been here two years. I don't remember much from when I lived over in Greenway if you're going to ask me about Rebecca Waters again."

"No, I was actually going to ask you about her parents. They seem unusually interested in me and what I'm doing."

"Just small town curiosity." Then he added, "It must be catching. You've only been here a couple of days and you're full of questions."

"Maybe, but I'm only curious in answer to everyone else's curiosity, so it doesn't count." She added thoughtfully, "Evelyn wants to come over for coffee someday. She said she wanted to talk about Rebecca."

"Probably not a good idea if you're planning to stay around. For all her quiet appearance, she strikes me as a needy sort of person. I imagine, if you start to make friends with her, you'll find out you'll be her only close friend."

"That's what I was thinking. I feel so sorry for her, losing a daughter like that and never knowing what happened to her, and also for having to live with Bill, but I don't think it would be a kindness to encourage her and then have to figure out a way to make her go away."

"So you're planning to stay around?"

"Not necessarily. But, even if I don't stay, I'll still be spending a lot of time here tidying things up."

"Town gossip has you staying."

"I'll bet it started with Jack, my persistent real estate man."

"Which is funny if you think about it. You'd think it would be in his interest to have you leave. It would give him another listing."

"What do you think Tara Leigh wanted to talk to me about? Are you sure it was me?"

"No idea, but it was definitely you. Her husband said 'Greg's little sister.'"

"Oh yes, 'what's her name.' Well, it can't have been about much if she didn't bother to look up my name." Taylor felt a little miffed that Tara Leigh hadn't remembered her name. After all, Taylor had remembered hers.

Andrew stood and set his chair back carefully in place, not moving toward the door.

"Is there something else?" She looked up at him, his rather imposing form standing still as though he was on the brink of a decision.

"Actually, there is." He cleared his throat. "I wonder if you would have dinner with me tomorrow night. If you want to miss the town gossip, we can go over to Greenway."

"Oh." Taylor felt at a loss for words. But why not? Relieved to realize she hadn't said those words out loud, she added, "Yes, that would be nice. Thanks."

"Pick you up at six tomorrow then." He was out the door

before she had come to terms with the fact that she was actually going on a date, with a policeman of all people. Andrew seemed to make a habit of speedy exits. She looked out the window, and he was already turning onto Main Street.

She wasn't going to tell anyone about her date, but then Edie called and asked her if she wanted to come over for homemade lasagna tomorrow. Taylor remembered Edie's lasagna with a great deal of affection and felt a little resentment toward Andrew for making her miss it.

"I'd love to, Edie, but I can't. I have to go out tomorrow night." No sense giving all the details, even to Edie.

"That boy is a fast worker."

"Who?"

"I just saw the police car drive down the street, so I think I'm justified in making a connection between that and your dinner plans for tomorrow."

"I'm not sure I did the right thing in accepting, but he caught me off guard and I said yes before I realized the significance of the question."

"And what is the significance of the question? A lovely young man has asked you out. Why would you have a problem with that?"

"Well, put that way, he is rather nice, not bad-looking too. But I don't want to start something I might have to finish if I decide not to stay."

"Correct me if I'm wrong, but he asked you on a date, didn't he? Did I miss the marriage proposal in there?"

Taylor laughed. "Okay, okay. It's just a date. I'm making too much out of it."

Chapter Seven

She leaned slightly to restore her balance. Too much! She tried to lean back the other way. She moved her foot to lose the snag from the knothole and stretched it out in front of her. She felt for the beam and came up with...nothing.

The next morning, Taylor decided to take a break from cleaning and organizing and get some of her own work done. Tristan, tired from a long walk, curled up at her feet. Denver, after a couple of walks across her keyboard, was persuaded to take a seat on the armchair where he sat glaring at her for his ignominious removal until he fell into a catnap.

About an hour later, she heard a knock at the door. She looked up at the clock. It was too early for Jimmy to be coming about the locks. Hopefully, it wasn't Jack again! She wanted to ignore the door, but her Jack Russell never let a footstep on his home turf without comment, so she had to get up to answer.

A total stranger stood looking at her. "I'm sorry to bother you, but are you Taylor Armstrong?"

Encouraged by the lack of pamphlets in his hands, she said, "Yes, I am. What can I do for you?"

"I'm Trevor Bridgeman, Tara Leigh's husband."

"Oh, I'm so sorry. Come in, please." She shushed Tristan and ushered Trevor into the living room where she removed Denver from the chair. At this second insult of the morning, he swished his tail and set off for parts unknown.

"Would you like some coffee? Or tea?" She was relieved

when he declined. The coffee was probably old by now anyhow.

She took a seat on the couch, turning expectantly toward him.

"I know this may seem like an intrusion, but Tara Leigh's death was such a shock. I'm trying to get my head around it, and I can't."

"Of course." Taylor felt the usual discomfort when dealing with the grief and loss of someone she didn't know, but she was finding it difficult to understand what he wanted from her.

"I know you're wondering why I'm here. It's a bit presumptuous on my part, but could you tell me what Tara Leigh wanted to talk to you about?"

"Trevor, I honestly don't know. You're the second person to ask me that, and I have no idea. I didn't really know your wife. We were different ages and in different grades at school."

"But, what did she say to you?"

"Nothing. I never saw her."

Trevor slumped back into his seat. "I thought you might have some sort of clue as to what is going on."

"Have you talked to Andrew, I mean, to the police? They should have some idea of what happened."

He snorted. "They have no clue. The doctor said she had a high level of alcohol in her blood. That's what they're saying happened. She got drunk and took the car out and drove right into the lake. That's totally ridiculous."

"Isn't it possible she ran into some old friends, and they had a drink together?"

"No!" he said rather explosively. "That's what that fool of a coroner thought. All he said was she had too much alcohol in her blood to be driving and some stupid recommendation to post more signs on the curve in the road. Tara Leigh didn't drink. She hasn't for years." Obviously noticing Taylor's sceptical look, he explained. "Tara Leigh had a drinking problem. We nearly divorced in the first years of our marriage over it. She quit with some help, and she hasn't touched a drop in nine years. She was proud of her accomplishment. She was really active in helping others with substance abuse problems. She would never touch alcohol. There has to be some explanation for what happened."

Other than to tell him that the medical results wouldn't lie, which obviously he wouldn't listen to, Taylor had no idea what to say to the man. He didn't seem to be in a listening mood. This altruistic Tara Leigh who helped others with their problems seemed a bit of a stretch from the Tara Leigh she knew, but then people changed. *Look at Greg.*

He leaned in and peered intently into her face, as if he were about to give her a personal lie detector test. "You're positive she never called you, or left a message, or a note?"

"I'm positive," said Taylor with as much firmness as she could muster. Why was it that, if she thought people believed she was telling a lie, she manifested all the physical symptoms of telling one? In a moment, she'd be blushing. "I don't really understand what you think she'd want to see me about. Maybe it was about the dog? It was my aunt that originally ran the kennel. Oh, what about Felix? Edie has been boarding him. I imagine you'll be wanting to take him home with you."

He sighed. "I guess I'll have to, although I'm sure I don't know what I'll do with him. He was Tara Leigh's baby. I travel a lot, so I can't look after a dog on my own. I imagine I'll have to find him a new home."

"It's a shame. He's a lovely dog. I don't imagine you'll have problems giving him away."

"Oh, I won't be giving him away. I'll be selling him. He's a registered purebred, and I paid a fortune for him."

So, his concerns for his wife's death didn't transfer into sentimental attachment to her dog. But then, Taylor admonished herself, not everyone was a dog person. To Trevor, maybe he was just an asset to be unloaded, maybe even a painful reminder of his wife.

Trevor sat silent, but was making no move to leave. She felt uneasy in his presence, but knew she should be feeling compassion for the man instead of irritation. After all, he'd just lost his wife.

To break the silence, she said, "Do you and Tara Leigh have children?" Then she cursed herself for insensitivity. If they had lost a child or wanted one vainly, her question could trigger pain in a man already facing loss. What a stupid thing to say. Also, it was none of her business. She was grasping at straws to break the uneasy gloom that filled the room.

"No, we don't. I guess Felix was enough for Tara Leigh,

and I never really wanted any."

Whew, she'd dodged the bullet on that one. The silent curtain fell again. "Are you sure you wouldn't like a cup of coffee?" She fell back on the old hospitality platform, but realized, if he accepted, she would face even longer silence.

That seemed to prompt him to leave. He stood up and said, "No, thanks. I've taken up too much of your time. I have to go and talk to Jenny now."

Taylor almost felt like calling Jenny to warn her, but then maybe she wanted to see him. After all, he was the husband of her oldest friend, a different situation from Taylor's. And besides, what had Jenny ever done for her? She'd probably tackle her again about selling the house. It was best to stay out of it.

She couldn't get back into her work groove that had been interrupted, so she thought she might as well have an early lunch and get it out of the way before Jimmy came.

He arrived at ten past noon and spent no time getting down to the business of changing locks. When he poked his head into the living room to say he was through, Taylor took him on a tour, showing him the shed that needed tearing down, the windows needing to be replaced, and the yard work to be done. Taylor wasn't sure why she expected him to pull out a little spiral notebook and a yellow pencil to make notes, but she was surprised when he took some pictures with his cell phone, jotting down notes on a phone app. He requested her e-mail address and said he'd send her an estimate.

He asked for the key so he could check out the shed. "Forgot about that old well," he said. "Don't know why they didn't fill it in years ago. Guess your grandpa didn't trust the town water supply."

As she walked him back to the front, he gestured at the kennels. "What are you planning to do with those?"

"Edie is boarding dogs there. She took in her first customer this week."

"Oh aye, the doggie belonging to Tara Leigh, the girl that got herself drowned." He made it sound like almost an accomplishment on her part. "Heard he was a Boxer, that right?"

"Yes, he's a lovely dog, but I don't think her husband wants to keep him."

"Seems a shame. I used to have a Boxer once. Good guard dog, he was. Maybe he'll be looking for a home for him?"

"Probably, but I think he's an expensive dog."

"Might be worth it for the right dog."

Taylor hoped he wouldn't be inquiring about the cost of the dog until after he had done her estimate. She had a feeling the two costs could end up related.

She felt restless that afternoon. She felt an aching from the loss of her brother that she thought she'd put behind her. She considered pouring a glass of wine and wallowing in her grief for the two family members she had been closest to, but remembered her date. It wouldn't do to appear half-inebriated for her dinner date, especially with a policeman. She settled for a cup of Earl Grey instead.

She sat unmoving in front of her laptop, remembering the last time she'd seen Greg. He'd finished his third stay in a dry-out clinic shortly before, but it hadn't been long before he was back in the emergency ward of the hospital. She had sat beside him as he had rambled on, probably not aware of a word he had said. She recalled he kept talking about redemption and penance. Taylor had assumed he had been referring to his years of drug and alcohol abuse. She had tried to connect with him, to ask him what he had meant, but he had turned his face away and had become silent. The next day, when she had gone to see him, he had walked out of the hospital, had just slipped out with a group of visitors. He had never contacted her again, and two weeks later, he had died of an overdose.

She looked at the box at the end of the couch containing his journals. She wasn't in the mood to read them now. She didn't want to compare the sensitive, practical, and always together Greg who was part of her childhood with the one she had just remembered.

Lighter reading was called for. She rummaged through one of the boxes she had filled with books and found one of the original Nancy Drew books from her childhood, *The Secret of the Old Clock*. Taking it and her Earl Grey upstairs, she ran a bath, threw in a fruity bath bomb, and prepared for a relaxing soak. The combination worked because she found herself drifting off, dropping the book to the floor.

Sometime later, she heard a scratching at the door and realized the water was quite tepid now. She hadn't fallen asleep, had she? She was probably still running short after her wakeful night of the intruder. She toweled off, checking the time. It was still early. She dressed quickly as Tristan was obviously impatient.

When they got outside, she discovered her dog was capable of a good performance. He showed no interest at all in bathroom duties, merely darted along, sniffing and checking his p-mail. She decided she needed the walk as much as he did, so was happy enough to oblige. The slight breeze blew away the cobwebs in her mind that had formed while she lounged in the tub, and she realized she was hungry. She was going to set negative thoughts aside and enjoy her dinner out. Why not? Andrew was an attractive and agreeable man, and as Edie had pointed out, it was just a dinner date, so she was going to make the most of it.

Her immediate problem was what to wear. It wasn't going to be a dressy occasion, not a dinner in Greenway, which was a town much the same size as Badger Lake. She pulled out a pair of black pants and added a longish, teal-colored blouse that cinched in at the waist with a gold, large-linked belt. Black pants were appropriate for anywhere with anything, and the blouse added a small amount of glam without going overboard. She didn't want to send out the wrong signals. She pulled her dark brown hair back and up into a scrunchie that nearly matched the color of her blouse, wrapping it around and holding it with bobby pins. She wore black shoes with a bit of heel to give her some height. He certainly had the advantage on her there. Andrew was probably at least six-two. Taylor was only five-three in her bare feet.

She gave Tristan a last shot at a pee in the backyard, bringing him back in just as she heard Andrew's tires crunch on the driveway. She opened the door on his first knock.

He looked at her admiringly. "That color suits you. You look great."

She covered the confusion she always felt at compliments by admonishing Tristan to go lie down in his bed. He had a crate, but she usually left it open. He seemed to have matured to the point that he could handle her short absences without getting into trouble. She should only be gone a couple of hours.

"There's a new restaurant in Greenway. I thought we could try it?"

"I've only been in Greenway a few times. I don't think

I've ever eaten there, so I'll leave it up to you."

They drove in silence for a while, but it was a silence that felt comfortable, not like some first date silences where the couple struggled to find something to say.

When they pulled onto Main Street of Greenway, he turned at the first right and parked outside a one-story building that Taylor thought she remembered as the old Credit Union. The sign over the door said simply "Mike's." Inside, the restaurant was typically rural Manitoba with a mixture of booths and tables and a decidedly western influence on the decor. There was country music playing in the background, but it was low enough not to be intrusive. They sat in a corner booth, Andrew seating her first and then sliding in so that his back was to the wall. She wondered if that choice had to do with his policeman training or just personal preference.

The menu offered a few surprises. In addition to the usual steaks, chops, chicken, and fish and chips, there were a variety of pasta, salad, and seafood dishes. She opted for the pickerel. It had been a long time since she'd had lake fish.

The pickerel was delicious, the vegetables happily not overcooked, and the coffee as good as one from Timmy's. They didn't talk much as they ate, but when the plates were cleared and the coffee topped up, he said, "I know everyone is asking you this, but I'm going to risk it anyway. Have you decided what you're going to do with the house? I promise I'm not going to offer to buy it."

Taylor wondered if the question was just another way of asking how long she was staying in Badger Lake, but she decided not to delve into his motives. She tried to answer honestly. "My original intention was to fix the house up and sell it. Nothing has really changed my mind since."

She suddenly realized that her comment could be taken to have underlying meaning, and she grabbed her coffee cup to cover the blush she felt coming, taking a big swallow and unfortunately breathing as she did. She immediately fell into a coughing spasm, gasping for breath. Andrew slid beside her in the booth, patting her rather hard on the back, but she waved him away. "I'm all right," she said.

He returned to his seat and waited till she was able to speak again.

"Sorry, I'm all right, really, just horribly embarrassed." Her voice was still raspy. She took a swipe at her eyes with a tissue and tried to regain her composure.

"Good. I've never had to call for medics on a first date. I wouldn't want to start now."

Taylor gave a quick laugh, thankful he had a sense of humor and the wisdom to use it. Her embarrassment melted away. She pushed her coffee aside and took a sip or two of water instead.

"Would you like dessert? Or a brandy?"

She shook her head. "No thanks. It was a lovely dinner, but I couldn't handle another bite."

Andrew took care of the check, and Taylor made a quick restorative trip to the washroom. She was thankful she hadn't worn mascara or gobs of eyeliner tonight. Not too much damage was done to her face by her coughing fit.

The evening air was cool, and Main Street was bare. The only stores open were restaurants and the one convenience store that rented movies. Instead of getting in the car, they took a walk around the two blocks that constituted Main Street then back to the car.

"Why did you move away from Greenway? Or was it your family that moved?"

"My family moved when I was sixteen. My older brother, Gordon, went into the military. I had no interest in farming, so Dad sold the farm to a neighbor who wanted more land, and we moved to B.C. I went to school there and then joined the RCMP. Eventually, I got posted here. That's my story, short and sweet. What's yours?"

"Just about as short, not sure if it's as sweet. My mother died when I was about eight, and Aunt Grace moved in to my grandparents' house and raised Greg and me. Greg went away to college first, and I followed him a couple of years later. I have an apartment in Winnipeg and here I am, back in Badger Lake for the moment."

"What about your father?"

She grimaced. "He's been out of my life since I was four or five." *And he's not getting back into it now*, she thought. She wondered if her father was still at the motel.

"And your brother, Greg?"

"He died a couple of years ago."

"I thought that must be the not-so-sweet part of the story, since he wasn't here for the funeral."

"He died of a drug overdose."

"That's rough."

"I've never been able to understand it. Greg was the calmest, most together person I knew when we were kids. He was always the responsible one. I was the brat. And he would never talk about his problems. That's what hurt the most. He wouldn't confide in me. We were close as kids after our mother died. He was the big brother other girls dreamed of having. Then he just sort of drifted away. He never finished his first year of college. He bummed around, working a little here and there. Then he started getting really far off the rails and stopped contacting either me or Aunt Grace. He did a couple of stints in rehab. Each time, we thought that would be the time we would get the old Greg back. Then, when he went off the wagon again, it would be worse than before, as though he'd been saving up."

She stopped for a moment. She had never talked to anyone this much about Greg. She hadn't been able to bring up the painful subject with Aunt Grace, trying to spare her, and Aunt Grace had likely been doing the same thing. In any event, Greg had always hung between them, as silent and untouchable as he'd been in life.

Andrew didn't break the silence. Maybe he was waiting to see if she had more. Taylor liked that he didn't immediately begin to offer meaningless platitudes. Instead, they walked in silence down the other side of the street.

"I talked to him just a couple of weeks before he died," she finally went on. "Well, I talked. Greg rambled. He'd been brought into emergency at the hospital, and they called me. I never had the chance to say goodbye to him. I don't think he heard a word I said, but I like to think he knew it was me there. He just talked to himself, mainly, or to whatever demons he was trying to unload—a lot of mea culpa and talk of righting old wrongs. Then, after a couple of days, he slipped out of the hospital without being seen. Two weeks later, he was dead." She felt the tears starting to come, and she sniffled to stop them, but she couldn't. She fumbled for a tissue, and Andrew handed her one, still without comment.

After she wiped her eyes and managed to stop any more tears, she dared to look up at Andrew. His eyes held encouragement, understanding, and no judgment. For a moment, he reminded her of Greg, as he had been before the change.

"Thanks for listening," she said. "I'm afraid I haven't

been a fun date. Twice reduced to tears in one evening."

"It's not over yet, so let's try to find something diverting to do."

"Like what?"

"Well, considering my job, I don't think we can play nicky nicky nine doors. We can go to the pub and listen to some music, or we can go back to Badger Lake and walk by the lake and scare the fish, or we can just go for a drive."

"Let's just go for a drive. Show me where you used to live."

"Really? That doesn't sound diverting to me."

"It does to me. Come on. Oh, it's starting to rain. There goes the walk by the lake."

The rain came quickly, and they turned and ran for the car, racing like kids. By the time they drove off, Taylor was laughing, and for now, the sad curtain that was Greg had lifted a little.

By the time they were back in Badger Lake, Taylor looked at her watch and realized it was much later than she had intended getting home. She hoped Tristan and Denver, well mostly Tristan, had behaved themselves and not chewed anything.

The moment they pulled into the driveway, the hairs on Taylor's neck stood up. *Something is wrong, but what?* Then she remembered the only light she had left on was in the kitchen, but now the overhead light in the living room was on. Andrew heard her sudden intake of breath and said, "Problem?" Then, without waiting for an answer, he said, "You stay here." He ran toward the house.

Taylor was going to obey him until she heard a whimper. *Tristan!* She jumped out of the car and followed the sound. Tristan was crawling toward her on the grass. She cradled him without moving him too much and looked for the cause of his distress. She couldn't see any blood or any obvious signs of broken bones, but he was definitely in pain. Andrew came out, and he had changed from his role as her date to policeman.

"Someone was in your house, and this time, he didn't use a key. The glass in the back door is broken. He smashed in the pane and reached in to undo the lock. Next time your handyman comes, he's to give you a solid door, understood?"

She nodded, but wasn't too concerned about the house right now. "I have to get Tristan to a vet," she said. "He's hurt, but I don't know how badly."

Andrew pulled out his cell. "I have the vet's home number. I'll call her direct and tell her we're on our way. Here. Let me." He took off his jacket and made a sort of sling, which he pulled under Tristan, lifting him into the car slowly. "I should secure the house, but the damage is probably already done, so I'll take you and Tristan to the vet and come back here. Call me when you're done, and I'll come pick you up."

The vet was a young woman, not much older than Taylor, with long, straight blond hair, unusually dark eyebrows since her hair looked natural, and a pleasant, reassuring manner. She lifted Tristan to the examining table and ran confidant hands along his frame.

"Nothing appears to be broken, but he has a bruise on his left thigh. He also seems a little tender around his abdomen. I would like to keep him with me overnight and keep an eye on what he passes. I think he's just bruised, but I want to be sure his insides are functioning properly. What happened?"

"I came home and found someone had broken into my house. Tristan was outside on the lawn, whimpering."

"He probably tried to defend the house. Jack Russells don't back down from anyone. I would imagine someone gave him a kick or two, miserable brute." Her eyes flashed with indignation, and Taylor saw how pretty she was. She wondered at Andrew having her home number in his cell. Did they have, or had they had, a relationship? Or maybe he just had to call her in the line of duty on occasion. Then she scolded herself. *It's none of your business, Taylor. You're just out on a casual date with him, right?*

"I'll send you home now and give him something to calm him and relieve the pain. My guess is, in the morning, he'll be nearly his old self. Leave me your number and I'll call you."

Taylor scrambled in her purse for a pad and pen and scribbled down her cell number and the house number. She was so relieved she felt the prickle of incipient tears. *Not again!* Three times in one night was just ridiculous. She never cried normally. What was happening to her?

"I think I'll just walk home," said Taylor. "It isn't far."

"Not with someone out there burglarizing your house and kicking your dog, you're not. I've already texted Andrew anyhow. I did it while you were writing down your number. He's on his way."

"You're nearly as bossy as he is," said Taylor with a smile. "Must be something in the water."

"I guess it's an occupational hazard. Policemen and veterinarians get used to being in authority, and usually my patients don't answer back."

Andrew's lights flashed through the door, and Taylor gave Tristan a gentle cuddle and a pat. He licked her face, and his tail wagged. He seemed drowsy already.

"Oh," said Taylor when she had slid into the front seat. "I was so busy worrying about Tristan, I didn't check for Denver. I hope he's all right."

"I can guarantee that he is. When I was looking over the house, I saw a gray tail swishing under the couch where he was hiding. Besides, I haven't heard of too many watch cats. I'm sure he made himself scarce the minute the trouble started."

"Still, I'll be glad to get home and be sure."

Andrew walked up the path with her. "I don't think you should stay here alone until that door is fixed. You don't have any way to secure it."

"I could hammer a board or two across for now and call Jimmy tomorrow."

"Not good enough. You have two options. Either I sleep on your couch, or you stay with Edie."

"Oh, Edie's probably already asleep. I wouldn't want to bother her, and you must want to get home, too. I'll be fine."

"I've already talked to Edie. She's all set to look after you. It's either that or me on the couch. You choose."

"It is something they put in the water," she said, ignoring Andrew's uncomprehending glance. "Okay. I don't want to bother you, and if Edie is already awake, I can go there. I don't need to take Denver. I just need to be sure he's okay and put something over the broken glass so he doesn't jump out. He's fine as long as he has food, water, and a litter box."

She poked under the couch, trying to coax Denver out, but he wasn't ready to be convinced. When that didn't work, Andrew decided to take the direct route. He walked to the end of the couch, gave a heave, and lifted it up. Denver gave a savage flick of his tail and ran for the stairs. Taylor caught him just before he hit the steps. She could easily see that the only thing damaged in Denver was his dignity, so she set him down. He took off to nurse his insulted self.

Andrew tore one of the boxes she had picked up at the Co-op for packing and taped a piece over the hole in the door, while Taylor swept up the glass. "There," he said. "It won't keep a burglar out, but it will keep a cat in."

Edie was waiting for them with a pot of tea. Andrew declined and said he'd look in on them in the morning. He explained he wanted to check the house once more and see if the intruder had gone to the attic again. He said it could be worth doing a fingerprint check, especially on the ladder and attic. Taylor accepted the tea and hung onto the hot cup as though it could warm her spirits as well as her body. She felt slightly comforted by the familiar kitchen. It was always warm, uncluttered, and welcoming.

"What's wrong with me, Edie?" she asked after Andrew left. "Twice now, someone has broken into my home. Every person I meet wants to know when I'm leaving town. Bill Waters thinks my brother is in hell. Have I broken some taboo I don't know anything about?"

Edie sat across the table from her and reached over to grasp both Taylor's hands. "I know you're upset now and nothing seems to make sense, but it will. It always does."

"How?"

"I don't know yet, but if we sit down and approach the problem logically, we have to come up with answers. So, let's get a pen and paper and start writing down the things we know." Taylor wasn't sure if Edie was serious about finding answers or was just trying to distract her, but it didn't matter. It was a good idea, and she was ready to try.

"Okay, the first strange thing was the off-the-wall comment Bill Waters made about Greg at the funeral. I don't know if he's just striking out at someone or if he really meant something by it. Can anyone really take him seriously?"

"Put it down. He obviously hasn't gotten over the loss of his daughter, but we don't know what makes sense and what doesn't, so we have to consider everything. What next?"

"Well, about five minutes after Aunt Grace was buried, Jack Vandenberg told me he wanted to buy her house. I wonder if he ever asked her to sell."

Edie thought for a moment. "I'm sure he didn't. She would have mentioned it."

"So the first significant thing is the house only became important when I hit town. Why?"

"Then you had another offer from Jenny."

"I didn't really take her offer seriously. I figured she just had a boring day and was looking for a diversion. She probably thought better of it by the next morning. Still, it does seem strange."

"Then came your break-in, the first one."

"And that was really weird. The burglar never touched my laptop or anything else of value, even my purse was sitting beside the living room recliner." She just remembered that. "He only went up to the attic, where nothing of value has ever been. What sort of burglar goes into an attic?"

Edie was writing everything down religiously, Taylor noted. Then she stopped and scribbled with the pen. Not getting any results, she got up and tossed it into the garbage, reaching into a drawer for a new one. Funny, Taylor thought, that was a difference in style between Edie and Aunt Grace. If Aunt Grace had been looking for a working pen, it would have taken at least three junk drawers searched to find one. Edie always knew exactly where to put her hands on everything. They were different in so many other ways, too, so maybe opposites did attract. Her mind suddenly darted to Andrew with that thought, and she quickly returned her thoughts to Edie's answer.

"The sort that's looking for something in particular and knows where to find it?"

"But what?" Taylor was beginning to think making a list was futile. Nothing made sense. But yet, a prickling at the back of her mind made her press on. "Old books? Old furniture?"

"Tara Leigh coming back to town has to be considered unusual," said Edie. "As far as I know, she hasn't set foot in Badger Lake for years. And her visit-an-old-friend reason doesn't hold up. If she was so close to Jenny, she would have known about her kids' allergies."

"Edie, everything that's happened seems to have a connection with The Famous Four. That's what Greg and his friends called themselves. They borrowed it from *The Famous Five* of Enid Blyton. As for Tara Leigh, both Andrew and her husband, Trevor, think she came to Badger Lake to talk to me. 'Greg's little sister, what's her name' was the way she put it." Then Taylor remembered she hadn't even told Edie about Trevor's visit, so she briefly described the exchange to her.

"I think the whole thing must involve Greg somehow," said Edie. "But we can't ask him." She stared morosely into her tea.

"No, we can't ask Greg." Taylor had suddenly had enough of this exercise. Instead of taking her mind off Greg and her other woes, it had just brought it all back. She crossed to the counter and poured another cup of tea, gesturing to Edie with the pot.

"No thanks. That's my limit for tonight. Otherwise, I'll be up all night going to the bathroom. The perils of old age." She smiled a little ruefully.

They sat silently for a few minutes. Then Edie set her cup down carefully and looked at Taylor. "When are you going to get around to asking me about your father?"

Taylor looked up, startled. "Why would I do that?"

"That's what you began to ask me the other day, isn't it?"

"Yes, but how in the world did you know that?"

"Good old Badger Lake grapevine again. He's been stay-ing at the motel. The clerks there wouldn't know Desmond— Des—but other people in Badger Lake have longer memories. Jean, who cleans rooms there, recognized him."

Taylor groaned. "I was going to tell you about him, but then other things got in the way. And then too, I'm not sure how much I really want to know about him."

"But he came to see you?"

"Yes. He showed up on my doorstep, as calm as if he'd been away on a three-week vacation, not a twenty-some-odd-year furlong."

Edie sat silently, waiting for her to go on. Taylor guessed the teacher in her taught her when to ask questions and when to just listen.

"He never explained why he'd never contacted us, never explained even where he's been living or what he's been do-ing. He might be married again with a new family for all I know."

"Did you ask?"

"Well, no. I think he pretty well cut all ties when he went away, and I don't see any way to gather them up again. I don't want to. He seemed to think I might want to see him.

He said he's staying at the motel, and I can contact him there."

She stood up to gather her conflicting emotions and poured some more water in the kettle. That tea needed diluting.

"You were nearly part of the family back then, Edie. What really happened?"

"Did no one ever talk to you about it?"

"Only dribs and drabs. Mostly, when I asked a question about my parents, my grandparents or Grace steered me off in another direction. They didn't seem to want to talk about it, except to say my father was useless and at the foot of all Mom's problems. Is that true?"

"There is always more than one side to a problem. I knew your mother then since Grace and I were friends, and I spent a lot of time at the house."

"And?"

"There's no doubt that Des was a wild one when he was young. Everyone was surprised he didn't get into more trouble than he did. His parents were middle-aged when he was born and probably not up to raising a rebellious teenager. You never knew them?"

"No. I don't think so."

"No, I guess you wouldn't have. They're long gone now. I think they were dead before Des left town. Anyhow, when he and your mother met, sparks flew. Do you believe in love at first sight?"

"I don't know. I don't think so. Maybe." She banished the picture of Andrew that rose to the front of her mind.

Edie grinned. "A well thought out response. Well, if such a thing does exist, that's what happened to them. They were inseparable. Your grandparents couldn't stand Des. They already had their hands full with Helen. Your mother wasn't an easy teenager to raise either. She had her own kind of wildness."

"What do you mean?"

"Helen didn't intend to stay in Badger Lake. She wanted more out of life. She wanted excitement and danger. She liked fast cars, pretty clothes. Most of all, she wanted people to love her. She wanted everyone to love her."

Taylor pursed her lips dubiously. "That's not at all the picture I have of her."

"No, I don't suppose it is. Your grandparents doted on her. She was the golden girl. It never seemed to bother Grace, being second in her parents' affections. She doted on Helen, too. I think that was partly your mother's problem— too much doting and not enough real life. I think it was mainly because of the gap between the two girls. After Grace, your grandmother had two—no, three pregnancies, I think. They ended in miscarriages. So when Helen came along, it seemed a miracle to them." She stopped, apparently lost in thought, then got up to pour her untouched tea into the sink, rinsing her cup thoroughly before setting it on the drain board.

"Anyhow," she went on, "when Helen met Des, that wasn't the type of man the family wanted for Helen. They tried to make him go away, forbade her to see him." Edie snorted. "They should have known that wouldn't work. A little short on psychology, your grandparents were. Anyhow, Helen and Des just up and got married one day, went over to Greenway for the weekend and came back a married couple."

"And then?" Taylor prompted as Edie seemed to run out of steam.

"After a week or so of cold shoulder, the family decided to forgive what they couldn't forget and began to help out. They stayed here at the house for a while, then rented a house, and Des got a job at the hardware store. Des and Helen lived their life the way they wanted to with lots of running around and partying. Helen got pregnant with Greg, and that slowed her down for a bit. They were coping, but just barely. When you came along, the strain was beginning to show on the marriage. Neither one was ready for a settled life. They began to argue a lot."

"So, one day, my loving father decided he couldn't handle it anymore and took the easy way out?"

"No one knows exactly what happened the night he left. We heard Helen's version but not Des's. Helen knew how to get her family on her side and might have exaggerated a little. I know there was a big dustup, but if you want to know the whole story, you might have to bite the bullet and ask Des."

Taylor suddenly said, "You didn't like my mother much, did you?"

"It wasn't that I disliked her, Taylor. I didn't understand

her. And I didn't like what was happening to Grace."

"What?"

"Grace was always the forgotten daughter, and then she became the unpaid nanny. Your grandparents invited Helen and the two of you to live with them, but Helen took advantage of the freedom that gave her and lived much the way she had before she married. Grace took on the responsibility of raising you and Greg, because your grandparents weren't really up to it."

Taylor felt a pang. For the first time, she realized what Aunt Grace had given up for them. She thought of all the times she'd rebelled and told her aunt she had no right to tell her what to do, and she felt ashamed. Then came the other thought. It wasn't just her father. Neither of her parents had wanted her. She suddenly felt very alone.

"I'm sorry, Taylor. I thought about whether I should tell you all this, because I knew it would hurt you, but everyone has a right to the truth."

"I can't say I'm glad to hear it all. I probably knew all along no one wanted me, and that's why I never asked questions, but it still hurts to hear."

"What a silly idea! No one said you weren't wanted. Your grandparents loved you. Grace loved you. In her own way, Helen loved you and Greg. She just didn't know how to raise children. And I do remember seeing your father with the two of you on more than one occasion playing in the yard or taking you out. He looked as proud as punch when he took you downtown."

"Then how could he just walk away?"

"Why don't you ask him?"

"You think I should go see him? Do you think he has the right to expect to see me and tell me whatever he wants? I'll have no way of judging whether it's true or something made up to make him feel less guilty. He has no right to expect it."

"No, he doesn't, but maybe you do."

Taylor looked across at Edie, her eyes brimming with unshed tears. "I'll have to think about it," she said. "Maybe I could forgive him for leaving, but I can't forgive him for never coming back."

Taylor had talked more than she wanted to about her father and didn't feel as though she could face any more. She took her cup to the sink and rinsed it, setting it on the drain board beside Edie's, signaling the conversation was over.

Edie said, "Are you just about ready for bed? I put clean sheets on the bed in the spare room when Andrew phoned, and there's a set of towels at the end of your bed. I think I've had enough excitement for one day."

"Me too." Taylor was tired but not sleepy, but she wanted to get away by herself to think things over. Edie was kind and helpful, but Taylor really didn't want to share her thoughts, even with Edie.

She lay awake in bed as she knew she would. She cleared her mind of her father by concentrating on the other questions. If she assumed that Bill Waters' comment wasn't just rambling but meant something to him, there was only one possibility. She wondered if it had occurred to Edie as well.

Greg must have known something about what happened to Rebecca. That would answer so many questions. Greg had been sensitive, the type of person who felt responsible for everyone, even things that he couldn't control. He felt responsible for the environment, responsible for poverty in the Third World countries, anything that he cared about, really.

If he thought he knew some clue to Rebecca's disappearance that for some reason he couldn't divulge, it would eat away at him and fester. That explained why he had changed, why he couldn't live with what he knew, whatever it was, and the only way he could block it out was to drink and do drugs.

But, what did he know, and who would he protect? He would protect his sister or aunt, but Taylor knew nothing, and the thought of Aunt Grace being involved in Rebecca's disappearance was absurd. That left the other three members of The Famous Four. Which one? And what could they know? Had she gone away with someone, escaping from her confining life, and told someone about it? One of the four? Maybe it had been Greg she had confided in. If she had sworn him to secrecy, he would have felt compelled to honor his promise, even in the face of grieving parents, a worried town, and a police search. But how did that connect to the strange behavior of the other three members of the group? Perhaps she had told them all what she had been doing, but only Greg had taken it personally.

Taylor remembered the entries in Greg's journal—the entries where he talked about the enmity between Tara Leigh and Rebecca and how it seemed to be getting better, that the two girls were becoming friends. But it still didn't answer the rest of the questions. Sure, Greg would have felt responsible if he had known the whereabouts of Rebecca and had been unable to tell, but she didn't see Jenny, Jack, or Tara Leigh being consumed with angst over it. And why would they suddenly feel the need to circle the wagons, even to the point of Tara Leigh coming back?

Then she sat up suddenly. *Of course!* Greg's journals. That's what the intruder had been looking for. It was really the only reason someone would have gone into the attic. Somehow, they knew the journals had been in the attic. But the intruder hadn't found them, because Taylor had taken them downstairs and put them in one of the boxes at the end of the couch. The intruder hadn't gotten what he wanted and had to come back again.

Taylor started to get out of bed. She had to check and see if the journals were still in the box, but somehow, she knew they wouldn't be. Then she lay back down again, knowing she would have to wait. She couldn't risk waking Edie who slept just a wall away. It would have to wait till morning. Now she wished she'd read the journals and not put them aside for another day. Something in them was important enough for someone to risk housebreaking to get them, and Taylor was pretty sure it was something to do with Rebecca's disappearance.

Chapter Eight

"This is your fault."

"No more than yours. What are we going to do now? We have to call someone."

"We can't. We'll get into too much trouble."

"We can't just leave her here."

"Why not?"

"They'll know she was with us. We'll get the blame."

"Are you sure she's dead?"

"She has to be. She hit her head on that pointed metal thing."

"Why didn't you move it before she went up?"

"Why didn't you?"

Taylor slept poorly and woke early. She lay in bed, waiting to hear sounds from the other bedroom. Soon, she heard Edie stir. She was of a generation when people rose early whether they had work to do or not. As soon as she heard Edie leave the bathroom, Taylor got up and dressed quickly. She wasn't going to waste time showering this morning. She'd settle for a quick wash.

Edie already had the coffee dripping and was whisking some eggs to scramble. "I thought I heard you up," she said. "Eggs for breakfast? Or does your generation live on coffee and smoothies?"

"Eggs are fine," said Taylor. She'd thought last night about whether to tell Edie what she believed, or whether just to make a quick getaway to the house. She didn't want people to be accusing Greg of something when he couldn't defend himself, but she had concluded that Edie was almost family, and she really wanted someone to act as a sounding board. It couldn't be Andrew, so Edie was the best bet.

She waited until they were done with breakfast and the plates rinsed and in the dishwasher.

"I see you've done some thinking overnight," said Edie. "What conclusion have you come to that makes you look so glum?"

She might have known she couldn't hide anything from Edie. She had the same radar system Aunt Grace had had when it came to reading thoughts.

"It's the journals," she said. "Greg's journals. That's the only thing they could have been looking for. But I moved them, so they had to come back to look again. I have to get over to the house and check, but I bet they're gone."

"What could there be in Greg's journals that someone would want?"

"It's not what they want. It's what they don't want," said Taylor. "I started to read a couple of entries. Some of the ones I read were from just before Rebecca went missing. Greg was talking about how Tara Leigh was so mean to her, and then they started to become friends. I was going to read some more but never got around to it. I had been thinking a lot about Greg after the funeral, and I'd worked myself into a bit of a funk about him. I just didn't know if I could handle reading more. I was going to do it later when I felt better about things." She grabbed her purse with the house keys and headed for the door, stopping there to wait for Edie. "Let's go. I want to be sure I'm right."

Edie walked with her to the house, and Taylor went straight to the box where she'd left the journals. They were gone.

"I knew it. They're missing. Oh, I wish I'd read more. There must have been something in there about what happened to make Rebecca disappear."

"Like what?" asked Edie. "Don't you think they would have told someone at the time if she'd run off with a boyfriend or just plain run away?"

"Maybe they knew who she ran away with, and she swore them to secrecy. As kids, they would have felt they had to keep a promise. But now, as adults, they would know it looks bad and people will blame them, especially the Waters."

"Taylor, I don't think you've thought this all the way through. If Rebecca ran away, she would have contacted someone, sometime. Not too many people can manage to just disappear at will, especially not a child, especially not an innocent like Rebecca."

"Do you have a better solution?" asked Taylor a little belligerently. She liked problems to be solved and wrapped up neatly, and she especially wanted this one to go away. "Rebecca's disappearance has to have some connection to The Famous Four. Look at Jenny and Jack wanting me to sell the house. Maybe that's what they wanted all along—Greg's journals."

"I don't think either of them would buy a house just to get something inside. The burglary has solved that anyhow. Besides, how did anyone know you had his journals?"

"The restaurant! Remember the day we had coffee there? I was talking about what I found in the attic. I'm sure I mentioned the journals then along with the books, broken furniture, and..." She broke off. "That means someone that was in the restaurant that day is the intruder."

"I think you're right, but who? I'm trying to remember who was there that morning, but I go so often, it's a blur. I can't remember who I saw there that specific day. The people I'm remembering might be from a different morning."

Taylor screwed her eyes shut and tried to picture the restaurant that morning. Both the Waters were there. She remembered that for sure, because she had thought Bill was about to say something to her when Evelyn stopped him. Jack was there, too, and Jenny, plus about fifteen other townspeople. She counted out the ones she knew to Edie.

"But it didn't have to be one of them," Edie said. "Any one of them could have been repeating conversations to someone they met afterward or someone at home."

"I can't think Badger Lake is that short of conversational items that someone is going to stop a person on the street and say, 'Oh, did you hear? Taylor found some old journals of her brother's in the attic.'"

"Don't get testy. I was just citing the possibilities."

"I'm sorry, Edie. I didn't mean to sound snarky, but I wish I understood. I honestly can't picture any of those people up in my attic rooting around."

The gravel crunched, and Taylor nearly groaned. It was going to be Andrew, she knew. She had wanted time before she talked to him, because she wasn't sure how much she wanted to tell him.

He came in with a slightly sheepish grin, and she saw the reason pull up behind him in the form of Jimmy's truck. "Sorry, but I thought you might not get around to calling him for a while, so I figured I'd do it for you. I hope you don't mind."

Taylor did mind, actually, but she couldn't really say so without sounding ungrateful. He was looking out for her safety.

Jimmy nodded at them and went through to the kitchen with his tape measure. "Have to see if I can get something in town. Might have to order if the measurements are unusual." His voice held little assurance that he expected it to be simple. Not one of life's optimists, Jimmy.

"So," said Andrew. "Have you had a chance to look around?"

"We actually just got here," Taylor began, but when she looked at Edie's expression, she knew she was going to have to tell Andrew about the missing journals. "There was something missing this time."

"Well, what? If we know what's gone, it will help. We can look for it to turn up somewhere. It usually does."

"Not in this case," said Taylor. "The only thing missing are my brother's journals."

"You're sure?"

"I'm sure. I found them in the attic the first day I went up there to sort things out, and I brought them downstairs and put them in a box behind the couch. So the first time the burglar came, he didn't find them. Last night, he either figured it out or had more time to look since no one was home."

"And have you figured out a reason for someone wanting the journals?" he prodded.

"I didn't read all the journals myself, so I don't know for sure, but the couple of entries I did read were just kid stuff, talking about friends, who got along with who, and things like that." She trailed off, not meeting Edie's eye. She wasn't going to tell Andrew what she thought, only what she knew. And she knew very little.

"So, who knew about the journals? And who would have

known where they were?"

"The whole town, apparently. I mentioned them in The Northland when Edie and I went for coffee. As far as I'm concerned, whoever it is can have the journals. I just want to know who it was that kicked Tristan."

"Has Vivian called yet?"

"No, I'm going to call her now to see if I can bring him home." The ring of her cell phone stopped her from saying more.

"Hi, Taylor. It's Vivian Lane calling. I tried you at Edie's first since Andrew said you were staying there. Anyhow, as far as I can see, Tristan is just bruised. He'll be sore for a few days, but should be right as rain when the bruising heals. You can come pick him up any time. Just let me know if he has any difficulties."

"Thanks so much. I'll be right there." She turned to the others. "She says Tristan will be fine, and I can go pick him up now."

Jimmy stood with his hand on the door and said, "I'll let you know about the door."

Andrew followed him out, and only Edie looked as if she had more to say. Taylor made it apparent she wanted to be off, so Edie sighed and picked up her purse, following the others out. She looked back at Taylor and said, "Call me when you've picked up Tristan."

Taylor nodded, but thought, *Not till I can get my ideas sorted out first.* It was then that she suddenly realized Andrew and the pretty lady vet were on a first name basis, and he must have seen her last night since she knew where Taylor was staying. Not that it was any concern of hers.

Tristan was delighted to see her, his tail thumping against the side of the kennel. Vivian was seeing another patient when Taylor arrived, so she dealt with the assistant. Just as she had finished paying her bill, the vet came out of one of the examining rooms. "He's a brave little dog and a resilient one too," she said. "I can't see any signs of serious damage, and he passed a clear stool this morning. His urine is fine too. I would guess whoever kicked him either just caught him with the edge of their shoe or didn't kick too hard. If they had, there could have been internal damage."

"Thanks so much, Dr. Lane."

"Vivian, please. No one calls me Dr. Lane. The kids call

me Dr. Vivian and everyone else, just plain Vivian."

Not exactly plain Vivian. The vet looked very attractive in her white lab coat, which set off her creamy complexion and hazel eyes under those dark brows to perfection. Taylor was grateful to her and said so. She certainly wasn't going to feel jealous twinges after one date.

When she got home, she took out her pad again and made a new list. She wrote down people who could have been her prowler.

Jack was at the top of the list. He was Greg's old friend and probably knew what was in the journals. He also had expressed a little too much interest in the house. Then she thought of Jack's six-foot frame and his years as the school jock. If he'd kicked Tristan, he likely would have done a more thorough job of it. She shuddered at the thought, and Tristan stood up and laid his head on her knee. She stopped to give him a pat. "What would I do without you, Tristan, my friend? I'm certainly glad our intruder wasn't stronger." Tristan simply wagged his tail and gave her a hopeful look. Such conversations in the past had sometimes led to treats. She obliged and then sat down and took up her pen again.

Jenny had expressed an interest in the house nearly equal to Jack's. She was also in the restaurant the day Taylor had talked about cleaning and finding the journals. She was a lot smaller than Jack, and even though she had once been an athlete, she might have softened over the years. Maybe a woman would naturally temper the strength of a kick aimed at an animal. It was hard to picture her up in the attic rooting around in the cobwebs.

Tara Leigh was not added to the list. If she hadn't died, she might have been at the top of it.

Then there was Bill Waters. Somehow sneaking around in an attic looking for old journals didn't seem his style. He was more the confrontational type. But he couldn't be ruled out either.

She stopped and put down her pen. It didn't seem the style of any of them. And the question came back to why? Why would anyone be interested in the notes of a thirteen-year-old boy? The parts she'd read seemed quite ordinary, even the parts that mentioned Rebecca. There were no big revelations or hints of wrongdoing there. Maybe it had nothing to do with Rebecca. But then what?

There seemed to be too many coincidences since she'd arrived in town. Even Tara Leigh's death seemed strange. The coroner had thought it an unfortunate accident, but the timing seemed funny. And who called to lure her out at night to the lake?

Taylor decided she had to do some checking. The weakest link would be Jenny. She phoned her on the pretext of talking about the house. Jenny must have been out the door when she hung up the phone, because she was on the doorstep before the coffee had finished dripping down.

Jenny crossed her bare ankles, adjusted the caramel shorts she was wearing, and took an exploratory sip of coffee, her eyes on Taylor all the while.

"So, have you decided to sell the house then?"

"Not exactly," said Taylor.

"I must have misunderstood." She set the cup down with a jar, sloshing a little on the coffee table. "I thought that was why you called me."

"I just wanted to know a little more about what you planned to do with it. The house has been in my family for three generations, and I feel I would really like to know your plans before I make any decision."

"I thought I explained it all to you the other day. I want a project. The house would be redecorated in great taste and style and would be a credit to your grandparents."

Taylor nearly choked on her coffee. She was pretty sure Jenny cared squat about her grandparents. And any redecorating she did to the old house would probably send them turning in their graves. They were very traditional, and Jenny was bound to prefer an open concept, trending toward Scandinavian or other minimalist design.

"What sort of things would you change?"

"Well, for starters, I'd make the living areas more open, maybe take down that wall." She pointed to the one behind Taylor that separated the living and dining rooms. Taylor felt vindicated in her assumptions. "After that, I'd probably consult with an architect to see what changes would be viable."

Which probably meant she hadn't given any thought to it at all.

"What about the yard and the garden?" She swore Jenny jumped at the question.

"Oh, I'd get a gardener to do something with the yard."

"Of course, that old shed should come down too."

"Of course," echoed Jenny.

Now was the time to divert the conversation, Taylor thought as she offered oatmeal cookies that were refused.

"You heard about the break-ins I've had."

"Yes," said Jenny. "You've been the talk of the town."

Taylor knew Jenny would be dying to leave once the conversation turned away from selling the house, but she intended to try to get some information out of her.

"It was really funny." Taylor went on watching Jenny's face as she talked. "The first time, the intruder just went into the attic. He never went in the other rooms at all. What sort of burglar ignores the loot downstairs and rummages around in the attic?"

"Probably some weirdo high on drugs who didn't know what he was doing."

"Hmm. Maybe. I'm just glad he didn't get my brother's journals when he was up there. They have no value, of course. But, to me, they're important."

Now she was sure Jenny twitched. She wasn't going to tell her the intruder got them the second time. It could have been Jenny, one or both of the times. Now, there was a thought. Maybe it wasn't the same person both times. But that was a stretch. Two burglars in Badger Lake, both targeting her house?

"It was certainly sad about Tara Leigh," Taylor said.

"Yes," Jenny agreed without adding any thoughts. It was not going to be easy getting an opinion out of her.

"Have you seen a lot of her since she left town?"

"Not a lot. We kept in touch."

"Her husband is in town, or maybe he's left by now. Did you know him well?"

"Not very well." Jenny was getting antsy, twisting a gold bracelet round and round. Taylor saw a thin white scar poke out along her left wrist each time the bracelet turned.

Taylor decided to get any sort of response from Jenny, she'd have to be direct. "What do you think happened to Tara Leigh that night?"

Jenny looked puzzled. "Why, she went around the curve too fast and drove into the lake. That's what the coroner said."

"Yes, but what made her go there in the first place? It's

not the sort of place you go on your own at night."

"She had a phone call just before she left. She must have gone there to meet someone. What difference does it make?"

"Didn't you wonder why no one came forward to say they called her? And where were they when she drove into the lake?"

"I don't see that it matters. She's dead."

Taylor could see that it didn't matter to Jenny. Tara Leigh may have been her best friend once, but now she was dead, so it was over. "Did you answer the phone call? If so, you must have an idea. You'd at least know if it was a man or a woman."

"One of the boys, Jaden—I think—answered the call. He just handed the phone to Tara Leigh. He can't remember what their voice was like. He's just a kid, you know. They don't pay attention to things like that."

Neither do you, thought Taylor. She had to stop herself from sighing out loud.

House or no house, Jenny was at the end of her patience. She stood and said, "Let me know when you're ready to do a deal on the house." She was out the door as quickly as she could go.

Taylor wasn't much further ahead than before Jenny's visit. But then, she thought about the twitch she saw, or imagined she saw, when she mentioned the journals. Somehow, all the bizarre things that had been happening since she arrived in Badger Lake centered on The Famous Four and Greg's journals.

A knock on the door broke into her musings. Edie stood on the step, holding a plate with two cinnamon buns. "I always bake when I'm trying to think," she said. "So I made these."

Taylor put the kettle on and made some English breakfast tea to go with the buns. They were the kind Taylor remembered. Aunt Grace hadn't been much of a cook, but the one thing she had been able to make was bread and buns. They were sticky with butter and brown sugar and just the right amount of cinnamon, exactly like these. She had probably gotten her recipe from Edie, or vice versa. Still warm, the extra butter she spread on them melted into the freshness.

Conversation halted as they ate. Taylor wiped the remaining sticky sauce from her plate with the last bite of bun and leaned back in her chair, temporarily satisfied. If she stayed much longer in Badger Lake, she might have to shop for a new wardrobe in a larger size.

Edie brought her back to the problem at hand. "Did Jenny have anything further to add?"

"No," said Taylor, leaning her elbows on the table, the sugar elation from the cinnamon buns evaporated now. "She doesn't seem to care much about Tara Leigh's death. It's strange that her best friend from school dies mysteriously, and she seems so detached."

"You still think the drowning is mysterious?"

"I think it needs further explanation. I told you her husband, Trevor, says she didn't drink and has been on the wagon for nine years."

"People have been known to fall off."

"Yes," sighed Taylor doubtfully. "But he seemed so sure."

"He has to hang on to something. He's her husband."

"And no one seems to know who called Tara Leigh that night. You'd think the police would be interested in knowing."

"They are," said Edie. "They checked the phone calls into Jenny's number, and the call came from the old phone booth around the corner from the hotel."

"I didn't think there were any phone booths left in Badger Lake."

"Just the one, but it works."

"How did you know about the call trace?"

Edie waggled her gray brows mischievously. "I have my sources," was all she said.

"Come on, give."

"The girl who works in the dispatch office is the daughter of an old friend, and I taught her in high school. She sometimes tells me things she probably shouldn't. So don't pass it on."

"I won't. But that means anyone could have made the call."

"Not anyone," Edie said slowly. "But, by now, I'm sure no one could say for sure where they were when the call was made or who they saw that night. How's Tristan doing?" she asked, changing the subject.

"Vivian says he should be fine. He's a bit of a ham, though, and likes to milk it."

Tristan realized he was being talked about and slipped out of his bed to stand beside Edie and put his head on her lap, a "poor me" expression on his face.

"See what I mean?" said Taylor. "Don't give him any treats. He's a real con artist."

"I didn't bring Jasper because I didn't know if he was up to a little rough play, but he looks pretty good."

"He chased a squirrel this morning, then he came running back and suddenly developed a limp. It lasted all of ten seconds till he realized he wasn't getting any treats for being an invalid."

"I never had a chance to ask you how your date went with all the fuss about the break-in and Tristan."

"Not bad."

"That's it? Not bad?"

Taylor grinned. "Actually, it went quite well. We had a nice dinner and a drive to show me where he used to live."

"And?"

"And nothing. I liked him. We got on well, but that's about it."

She was saved further explanation by the crunch of gravel in the drive. Jimmy was here to change the back door. He was certainly faster than she had expected the only handyman in town to be.

"Lucky," he said, throwing down his cigarette on the gravel and grinding it out with his boot before coming in. "I found a door at the lumberyard with the right measurements. I'll pull around to the back and unload it. If it fits, I'll have it done this afternoon."

"Thanks, Jimmy. I appreciate it."

Edie was gathering up her empty plate when she got back to the kitchen. "I'm going to take Felix and Jasper for a walk."

"No word yet from Trevor on his plans for Felix?"

"He hasn't even checked up on him. I imagine he'll be leaving town after the funeral."

"I wish we could find out for sure if he came to town the day after Tara Leigh died."

"You think he had something to do with it? I don't see how he could have been in town. The police notified him by phone, and he was there to answer."

"Probably a cell phone number. He could have been anywhere."

"I can ask Phyllis at the hotel when he checked in. But if he didn't want to be seen in town, he would hardly have checked in to the hotel."

"Strange things happen. Maybe he followed Tara Leigh and they had a fight, something happened unplanned and he just hoped no one would check."

"Okay. I'll ask, but if Trevor and Tara Leigh had problems of some sort, why would they bring them to Badger Lake to sort out?"

"Like I said, maybe it just came up."

Edie grunted discouragingly and left Taylor trying to figure out whose movements she could verify for the night of the phone call. She wondered if she was trying to find connections to Tara Leigh's death that had nothing to do with Greg and his journals. It was possible the two things weren't even related.

She didn't have Edie's advantage of age-old friendship with people to get information in casual conversations. How could she find out where Jack, Jenny, and Bill Waters were on that night?

She took Tristan for his walk and then wandered down to the store for milk and vegetables. She was going to have to start cooking proper meals instead of relying on the one-person frozen dinners in Aunt Grace's freezer.

Coming out of the store with her bag, she nearly bumped into Evelyn Waters. Evelyn did a complete turn around and walked out of the store beside Taylor.

"How about a cup of coffee," she said to Taylor. "We've never had a chance to talk, and, if you're planning to stay in Badger Lake, we should get to know each other. After all, I was friends with Grace."

Taylor ignored the comment about her staying in Badger Lake. She wasn't going to answer anyone's queries about how long she was staying. As far as being a friend of Aunt Grace, Taylor couldn't remember anything in her visits home to support that story. Oh well, she was going to have to talk to her sometime, so she might as well get it over with.

"Coffee would be nice," she said. "I don't have anything too perishable in here. Shall we go to The Northland?"

"Let's go to my house instead. Everyone in the coffee shop listens to everyone else's conversations."

Don't I know it, thought Taylor. Anyhow, going to Evelyn's house gave her the advantage of being able to leave when she wanted, much better than inviting Evelyn into her home.

The house was small and old-fashioned, but the garden was filled with sweet peas and marigolds and some tall, blue flowers Taylor didn't recognize. Gardening had never been a priority in their household. Inside, the kitchen was almost painfully clean. It made the room lack the warmth usually associated with kitchens. Yet Edie's kitchen was just as tidy and still managed to keep the feeling of comfort that greeted everyone who entered. She could see into the living room, a tidy room with a small television under the window and crocheted doilies everywhere on the many side tables and on the backs and arms of the chesterfield and chairs.

Evelyn busied herself making the coffee and setting out a plate of homemade matrimonial squares. Taylor felt a pang for the loneliness of the woman with no family to bake for and no grandchildren squealing around the rooms with sticky fingers to muss up the carefully arranged furniture. A husband like Bill was surely cold comfort. She wondered if Evelyn felt the same passion for religion as her husband. It was difficult to tell. Apparently, she attended church regularly, but without the fiery testimonies of her husband. Her face was so calm it was difficult to tell what went on behind the gentle smile.

No one spoke as Evelyn set out the china cups and the matching cream pitcher and sugar bowl. The silence seemed oppressive to Taylor, but her mind went blank when she tried to think of a conversation starter. Finally, Evelyn poured the coffee and sat down. Taylor intended to make her excuses and leave as soon as possible.

"It's so nice to have an Armstrong back in town," Evelyn said. Again, that implied question about her staying was there, or was Taylor imagining it? "Everyone misses Grace. We were all sorry she was taken so young."

"Thank you," said Taylor.

"And your brother, Greg, you must miss him a great deal."

"Yes," said Taylor simply. She wasn't going to get into a discussion of Greg with Evelyn or any other stranger.

"He was friends with our Rebecca."

"Yes, I can remember seeing her around. She helped me with my homework once."

"She was so fond of Greg. She used to talk about him all the time. And that Tara Leigh." Her face puckered up as though she had swallowed undiluted lemon juice as she said the name.

"I was never really close to Tara Leigh," said Taylor. "To her, I was just the annoying little sister."

"Did Greg talk much about Rebecca? After he went away, I mean."

"I never really saw too much of Greg after he left home. He had his own interests, and I was busy finishing school and then college. Our visits were pretty short and far between."

"Yes. It was so sad how he let himself be taken down by the abuse of drugs and alcohol. Some people have little resistance when something preys on their mind."

Now Evelyn was starting to sound a little like her husband. Taylor had a sharp retort ready, but was saved from needing it by the arrival of Bill through the living room entry. He walked to the counter and poured a cup of coffee. Then he opened the cupboard beside the stove, the one that had held the squares, reached toward a tin container marked Tea Biscuits, stopped in mid-reach, and frowned.

"The bottle," he said. "Where's the bottle?" He turned to look accusingly at his wife, and somehow, Taylor felt included in the accusation.

"What bottle?" asked Evelyn. Then, "Oh, that bottle. I don't know. I haven't thought about it in ages."

Bill turned and stormed back the way he came in. "Someone must have misplaced it," he fumed. Since the only someone he shared the house with was probably the only someone to have access, Taylor watched Evelyn's face for signs of distress. She saw only Evelyn's usual placid demeanor. She must have been used to his outbursts.

Taylor looked puzzled enough that Evelyn must have felt an explanation was necessary. "Bill has had a bottle sitting in the cupboard for years. When he was much younger, he drank. He keeps that bottle as a reminder of the evils of drink."

"Oh." Taylor had heard of people doing such things, but she thought it was an invitation or a form of self-imposed torture, whatever way you looked at it. "But how could it go missing?"

Evelyn gave a slight shrug. "Who knows? It's been there for so long, it might have been taken by a visitor ages ago."

Taylor thought visitors were a rare enough occurrence at the Waters house that the list of possible culprits should have been easy to narrow down. Then she said, "Do you suppose someone broke in while you were out? If they broke into my place twice, maybe they've picked other houses, too. But, what a strange thing to take, just like the jour—" She stopped. She didn't want everyone to know what had gone missing.

Evelyn gave a brittle smile and said, "People are becoming less trustworthy these days. It could have been a burglar." She made no comment on Taylor's unfinished sentence.

"If it was the same burglar," said Taylor, sensing an opportunity to find out Evelyn and Bill's whereabouts. "Then maybe it was the same night. Were you home then?"

"Which night would that be again?"

"The first break-in was the night before Tara Leigh died."

"Oh yes, that was prayer meeting night. We would have been at church."

"I was," said Bill. He had just popped into the kitchen again to refill his coffee cup. "You weren't feeling well and stayed home." He said it in an accusing tone, as if implying Evelyn had purposely felt ill to shirk her duties as a church-going woman. Then he stopped. "Prayer meeting wasn't the night before that woman died. It was the same night."

"Oh yes, I get dates mixed up sometimes. I remember now. I had a bad head. I get them from time to time and have to take medication and lie down."

"Hmph!" Bill disappeared again. He was like the Energizer Bunny, the way he couldn't seem to stay still for long.

Bill could have been the burglar. He was certainly fit for his age and could move fast. His prayer meeting alibi wasn't for the night of the break-in, and she couldn't think of a way to ask more questions without seeming intrusive. But he was out the night Tara Leigh died. Jenny said the phone call was just after nine. She thought the prayer meeting started at eight, but could it have been over by then? Bill was the long-winded one. If he'd wanted to, he could have shortened his usual spiel and been out in time to make the phone call. Then, if Evelyn had been asleep, she wouldn't have noticed he was away, and he could have met Tara Leigh. It sounded a bit far-fetched, but was certainly a possibility.

She wanted to think it over alone. Then she would call Edie and see what she thought.

She quickly emptied her coffee cup and stood up. "I'd better be heading home now. I need to get my groceries put away and take Tristan for his walk."

"Tristan? Oh yes, your dog. How is he doing? I'm not fond of dogs, but it seems a shame the poor little thing was injured."

"He's doing fine." Some of Taylor's sympathy for Evelyn disappeared at the admission she didn't like dogs. How could you empathize with a person who didn't like dogs?

"Have another cup of coffee," Evelyn persisted. "The groceries can wait. Our conversation got interrupted."

Taylor nearly said, "Thank heavens." But she merely smiled and said firmly, "Sorry, I have to go. Maybe some other time?" she added to soften her departure.

She couldn't wait to get home. The visit with Evelyn had left her depressed. What a lonely life the woman had. But it wasn't up to Taylor to bring companionship to her. So why did she feel guilt that she was so happy to get away?

Chapter Nine

"Okay, listen. Remember that girl from Greenway? The one who went missing?"

"What about her?"

"They never found her. They think she ran away. What if they thought the same this time?

"We can't do that."

"Why not?"

"Her parents. We have to tell them."

"You want to try to tell the police what happened then? They'll arrest us and throw us all in jail till we're old."

"They wouldn't do that. We're not grown-ups."

"Well, we'd go to juvie until we're old enough to go to jail. We'd never finish school, never play ball again, never."

"Okay. Okay. What can we do?"

"We have to think."

Taylor spent the afternoon organizing items for sale and to keep. She'd been putting off going back into the attic, but decided it needed to be done, so she spent a dusty hour or so sorting boxes and hauling some of them downstairs.

She didn't realize how much time had passed until her stomach started rumbling, and she realized she hadn't eaten anything since the matrimonial bar at the Waters'.

She washed and threw a frozen dinner in the microwave, filling Tristan and Denver's dishes while she waited. So much for her plans to cook proper meals. Tristan had nearly finished his dinner when the microwave pinged, but with a full stomach, he wouldn't be inclined to beg. It was much easier to eat a meal undisturbed if the four-legged family members were occupied.

After her dinner was cleared, Taylor couldn't get back in cleaning mode, so she fell asleep on the couch watching re-runs of *Friends*, waking up with a start at ten o'clock. She strained to hear if there had been a noise that woke her, but all was silent. Tristan dozed at her feet, so she brushed her teeth and went to bed properly.

The next morning, after breakfast and a walk, she was mellowing with her third cup of coffee when she looked out the window and saw Edie heading downtown with an empty shopping bag. She hailed her through the living room door and invited her in. Edie complied quickly to her invitation.

Taylor was already full of coffee, so she put the kettle on for tea instead.

"It looks as though my boarding kennel days are over for the time being," Edie said as she swirled hot water around in the teapot. Taylor was never that fussy and didn't see what difference a warm pot made anyhow, but Edie was old school with her tea.

"Trevor came by to pick up Felix?" she asked.

"Yes. He says he's going to sell him and already has a buyer."

"That sounds like he's staying in Badger Lake—the dog, I mean."

"He didn't say who he sold him to."

"I can make a guess. If I'm right, my handyman's bill just went up."

Edie chuckled. "You could be right. Jimmy used to have a Boxer. I know he's partial to them, and I've heard him say he'd like to get another dog."

"Did you find anything out about Trevor's whereabouts the night before he officially hit town?"

"As far as I can tell, he arrived when he said he did, unless he slept in the car. He didn't check into either the hotel or the motel." Edie checked the tea and set the pot back down.

"Oh well, that's one avenue of investigation we can close."

"I had coffee with Evelyn yesterday afternoon," Taylor said, eyeing the pot. She didn't like tea as strong as Edie did.

"And how did that go?"

"She makes a very nice matrimonial square. It tastes a lot like yours."

"Where do you think she got the recipe from? Did you learn anything new?"

Taylor told Edie about her conversation with Evelyn and Bill and about the missing bottle. "So it seems like we have a burglar in town," she finished. "Maybe it was just a coincidence he came to my place."

"You don't really think that, do you?"

Taylor sighed. "Not really. Not when he specifically targeted the attic and came back a second time. There's no doubt it was the journals he was after. I just wish I hadn't been so slow to make the connection. I could have hidden them."

"We're always so much cleverer in retrospect. Did you find out where Bill was during the time of the burglary?"

"Nothing for the night of the burglary, but Tara Leigh died on his prayer meeting night."

"So Bill's whereabouts are accounted for," Edie said as she gave a taste test to the tea and set the pot back down once more to steep a little longer.

"Not really. The phone call was just after nine. He could have been out of prayer meeting in time to make the call."

"But Evelyn would have asked why he wanted to use a booth to make a call."

"Evelyn wasn't with him that night. She had one of her headaches and stayed home. She says she fell asleep, which means she didn't know what time he came in. He could have met Tara Leigh."

Edie went back to their earlier conversation, "Bill hasn't drunk since just before he and Evelyn got married. Why would he have a bottle of liquor in the house?"

"Apparently, it's there as a reminder of the evils of alcohol. It sounds rather silly to me." Taylor decided the tea was strong enough and poured out two cups. Edie added milk and sugar to hers, but Taylor had always drank tea as she drank coffee—the way it came out of the pot. She took a tentative sip and decided if she was going to be drinking tea with Edie, she might as well learn to dilute it. The tea was much too strong for her preference.

"Do you think the missing bottle has any connection to your break-ins?" Edie asked.

"I don't see any connection. We know my burglar was looking for Greg's journals, because he took them. Well, correct that. We know the second burglar wanted the journals. The first one might have been a different person. But then, why target the attic? No, it must be the same one." She thought for a moment and went on. "As for the bottle, it seems a coincidence. We have two break-in artists in Badger Lake at the same time."

"I wonder..." said Edie.

"What?"

"I wonder if Bill could have taken the bottle himself. Maybe he had a fall off the wagon."

"He wouldn't have brought the missing bottle to our attention if that was the case. And he definitely acted put out about its disappearance."

"Could Evelyn be a closet drinker? She's lived all her life in Badger Lake, so she'd have to be pretty good at hiding it, but some people seem to be able to."

"If so, surely she would have covered her tracks and replaced it."

"Maybe she didn't have time."

After Edie left, Taylor sat for a while, trying to remember anything about her father before he had left them. She couldn't picture him as anything other than the man who appeared on her doorstep out of the blue. Her mother died two years later, and she could barely remember her.

Tristan sat down on his haunches beside her and nosed at her hand, whimpering softly. She patted his head. "Dogs are so much more reliable than people, don't you think, Tristan? You never lie, well, maybe on occasion when you insist you never had enough dinner, but that's just a white lie. Time for a walk. You need to go out, and I need to clear my head. Go get your leash." She pointed in the direction of the door. Tristan needed no more encouragement. He came back with his leash and pushed it toward her.

Taylor decided to walk a different direction this time. She hadn't really taken a chance to walk or drive the side streets and see the changes in Badger Lake since she'd left. Following Second Avenue past the seniors' residence, the Waters came out of the building, headed toward her.

It was too late to cross the street without making her avoidance obvious. Instead, she pasted a smile on her face, said a brief "hello," and continued walking, intending to pass quietly. She was startled to discover Tristan had other ideas. As the Waters approached, he began a low rumbling in the back of his throat, which escalated to a growl as they met. She pulled him up sharply on his leash. "I'm sorry. Tristan isn't usually like this. I guess he's sensitive to people he doesn't know after his accident."

Evelyn waved her explanation aside. "Oh, that's all right," she said. "Dogs never like Bill anyhow."

Taylor saw why. The little man was a mass of nervous energy, not the type of personality likely to make canine friends.

Still, she thought about Tristan's reaction as they walked. Could he have been trying to tell her something? Bill was one of the people who could have been the intruder that had injured him. She thought maybe she'd test it out on another occasion and see if Tristan still reacted that way to Bill Waters.

She was busy with her musings and suddenly realized she had walked all the way to the east side of town. The motel was no more than a block away. Maybe her subconscious was trying to make a point.

After spending far too much time trying to decide what to do about her father, Taylor concluded the only way to get him out of her thoughts would be to actually visit him and listen to what he had to say. She didn't have to accept it, just listen to it. Then she could tell him to go his way, she never wanted to see him again. The conversation might act as an exorcism to get out some of the old pain. Now would be a good a time as any. She had Tristan with her, and she could test out his reaction to her father and see if he growled at him too. There was always the possibility that Des had wanted something from the house and had broken in, although she couldn't think what it would likely be. Maybe the only reason he visited her was a reconnaissance maneuver.

She walked around the side of the motel and stood for a moment in front of door 16. Then she squared her shoulders, tightened her grip on Tristan's leash, and knocked.

The door opened almost immediately. She wondered if he had spent his days waiting for her to come, but pushed the thought aside. She wasn't going to be swayed by sympathy for a lonely man who was the author of his own problems.

"I'm glad you came," he said simply, and stood aside for

her to enter.

Once inside, Taylor wasn't sure how to start. She looked around at the slightly worn furniture of the room, taking in the coffee cup sitting on the marked table and the lone suitcase on the folding luggage holder. She smelled fast food and saw takeaway containers in the garbage.

He gestured to one of two armchairs in the room and asked, "Coffee?" There was a mini coffee maker on the desk surface along with some tea packets and two more clean cups.

"No thanks," said Taylor. "I'm not staying long."

He nodded and waited for her to sit before taking the other chair.

"I just wanted to give you a chance to explain, and then it's over," she said. "Then you can go off to wherever you've been for the last twenty years, and I can get on with my life."

"Fair enough," he said. "Where would you like me to start?"

"With the night you left," she answered.

He leaned back and closed his eyes for a moment before beginning. "Your mother was a beautiful woman," he began. "Helen was full of life and seemed to always want more of it. She loved music and dancing and had a craving for other people's admiration. I don't know why, but I remember one time—"

"The night you left?" Taylor interrupted.

"You sure you want to hear it?"

"Not really, but I don't think you've left me much choice."

"I was working late at the hardware store that night. We had to do an inventory and usually that kept us till midnight. Johnny, the owner, got some food from the restaurant, and we ate after we were done. We had finished earlier than usual, so it was only around ten when I headed home. I thought you and Greg would be in bed and Helen might be watching television waiting for me." He stopped and cleared his throat before continuing. "I heard the music as I drove up, and there was a car parked in the driveway. I didn't recognize it at first. When I opened the door, there was Helen, and there was Rod, a man I thought was a friend." He looked at Taylor as though checking to be sure she understood what he meant.

She said nothing.

"I went sort of crazy, I guess. I started punching him and couldn't stop even with Helen pulling me, trying to get me off him. Finally, when I stopped to take a breath, I realized he was just lying there, not moving. I didn't know what to do. Then he kind of snorted. I hadn't killed him. Helen called her parents, and they came rushing over. They told me to go to their house and stay there, and they'd look after everything. Well, they did, but not in a way that was for my benefit. They got a friend to clean up the mess and arranged to get Rod out of town to a hospital where they took care of everything he needed."

"Did he recover?"

Des shrugged. "I never saw him again, but according to what I was told, he eventually recovered."

"So?"

"So, when Helen's parents, your grandparents—"

"I know who they are." Taylor didn't feel like making things easier for him.

"When they came home, they told me Rod was in the hospital. The doctor said he'd be all right in time, but that I'd hurt him pretty badly. They also had a paper with them. It was all typed out with what happened that night, and they got Rod to sign it, saying what I'd done to him. Then they told me he wasn't going to press charges. They'd worked some financial magic for his silence, but I had to leave Badger Lake and never contact Helen or you or Greg again. If I ever did, they'd charge me and I'd go to jail, perhaps for a long time."

Taylor snorted. "Oh come on. People have killed and gotten away with a few years in jail. What do you really think would have happened?"

"I couldn't take that chance. Then, too, I didn't want to drag Helen through all the gossip-mongering. I didn't want to do that to her."

"Very noble, I'm sure. The town must have known what happened. If you burp in Badger Lake, the rest of the town knows in five minutes what you ate for breakfast. How could they hide that?"

"I don't know, but they did. I think Rod went to Winnipeg to be treated. He was supposed to be leaving town with his family anyhow. Everybody believed your grandparents, so whatever they said was taken as truth."

Taylor stared at him for a few minutes, not speaking, wondering how much of what he said was true. She had no way to find out. She didn't know this Rod person, and, if she did, she could hardly go to him and ask, "Did you sleep with my mother once and make my father beat you up?"

"So, where did you go?"

"I headed to the west coast, worked on the island in a lumber camp for years."

"And you never tried to get in touch?"

"I was afraid to. Your grandparents weren't the type of people to back down or change their minds. If I came back, I was positive I would have been in jail."

"You must have heard what happened to my mother. Didn't you think to come back then to care for your orphaned children?" Taylor threw as much scorn as possible into her question.

"I thought that would have made your grandparents even more anxious to keep me away."

"And when they died?"

"I heard about your grandmother, but didn't know your grandfather had already died. I wrote a letter once and mailed it to him. It came back. It wasn't marked deceased. It just said undeliverable or something like that, so I thought nothing had changed."

"Why did you come back now?"

"I heard about Grace. That's when I realized your grandfather had died too. I thought no one would stop me with the last of the family dead."

"You didn't break into the house a few nights ago, did you?"

He looked startled and said, "No. Why would I do that?"

"To look for the paper with the account of the beating and Rod's signature?"

"I don't think it much matters now," he said. "It wasn't the paper that was the problem. It was who had possession of it." Then he stared at her. "You don't have it, do you?"

"If I did, I wouldn't need to ask you what happened that night, would I?"

"No, I guess not. Anyhow, here I am." He gave her a rueful smile, but his sheepish look didn't do anything to make Taylor feel sympathetic.

"I still think you could have found a way to contact us.

You could have written a letter. We heard nothing when we graduated, when Greg—"

"I wrote a letter once. I addressed it to you and Greg, in care of Grace. I thought, if any of Helen's family had an ounce of forgiveness in them, it would be her. Either she was brainwashed by her parents, or maybe she never even got it. I wouldn't be surprised. Grace wasn't the kind to rely on other people's opinions." Des lowered his head toward his knees, and, for a moment, Taylor thought he was going to faint. Then he lifted his head and said, "I did see Greg once, you know."

"He would have told me."

"I don't think so. I doubt if he even knew who I was, even though I told him. I tracked him down to a rehab center, but when I saw him, he'd been released and had already fallen off the wagon. I couldn't make much sense out of what he said."

Taylor started, a memory striking her. "He knew you were there."

"Did he say something to you?"

"Not exactly, but one time, we were talking and he said, 'He finally came back, after all this time.' I thought he was talking about a friend of his and never paid any attention. But that must have been after he saw you." They both sat silently for a few minutes. Then Taylor jumped up and said, "I have to go." She had too much information and too much raw emotion to digest, and she had to get out of this room and away from her father's presence to think.

"Will you come again?"

"I don't know."

"Please." The word tore out of him. Through her own unshed tears, she sensed his pain. Part of her was glad and wanted him to feel pain. The other part felt something she didn't understand right now.

Tristan had been lying on the carpet between them, his eyebrows twitching as his eyes followed the conversation back and forth. Now he offered a small whimper as his contribution and stood up. He walked to Des and nuzzled his hand briefly before turning to Taylor and tilted his head, trying to understand what was going on.

"I'll see," she said as she grabbed Tristan's leash and headed for the door.

She walked rapidly, wanting to put as much distance as she could between her and the man sitting alone in his dingy room, trying not to feel sympathy for him, trying not to feel anything for him.

Tristan trotted along, not stopping to sniff fences and tree bases as he usually did, perhaps sensing that Taylor needed time to walk out her emotions.

Finally, she slowed, then stopped and reached down to scratch Tristan behind the ear. "Well, boy, we have a lot to think about, don't we?"

A car pulled off to the side in front of her, and she waited for Andrew to climb out, untangling his long legs from the front of the police car.

"I wasn't speeding, was I, officer?" She grinned, wanting to change her mood and hoping a little banter might work.

"I thought you might like a coffee?"

"Perfect. I'd love some."

"We can go to the drive-in. They have a few seats inside, and I think Tristan can slip in if he's quiet. I'll say he's help-ing police with their inquiries if anyone asks. Or, we can sit in the car."

"The car, I think. Tristan sometimes plays to an audi-ence. There's no guarantee he'll be quiet."

He turned the car and headed back to the outskirts of town, past the motel, pulling in to the drive-in lot. "Back in a flash," he said. "No cream, no sugar, right?"

"Yes," she said, taking a moment from darker thoughts to feel slightly flattered that he remembered she took it black.

When he came back a minute later with the coffee, he said, "Went to see your father, did you?"

She stared at him, amazed. "How did you know? I'm be-ginning to wonder why anyone ever takes out an ad in the classifieds in Badger Lake. Everyone in town knows what everyone else is doing and thinking."

Andrew smiled. "It's not quite as bad as that. You'd be amazed what secrets there actually are in a town this size."

She stared at him, unbelieving.

"Not that I'm going to tell you, of course, but not every-thing gets to be Northland gossip."

She thought back to the story Des had told her and thought maybe Andrew had something there. It seemed to be only the unimportant things that everyone knew. "My father?" she prompted him when he seemed to have lost the thread of conversation.

"Oh that. Actually, I talked to him on the phone last week. He said he was coming to town for a visit and wanted to make sure he had no legal problems to worry about. I told him there were no outstanding charges against him, and he thanked me. That was it. Then I saw his name in the motel register while looking on another matter."

They sat quietly for a moment. Taylor took a tentative sip of her coffee and set it down in the center cup holder. It was still much too hot.

"How did it go?" he asked.

She sat up quickly. "I just realized," she said, an accusing tone in her voice, "when we went for dinner the other night, you knew about my father. He'd already talked to you. And you didn't say a word to me about it."

"I'm sorry. Maybe I should have, but you were talking about your brother and were upset reliving his death. I did ask you about your father, and you didn't seem to want to talk about him. I didn't think it was the time to bring up another painful subject."

"Oh," she said. "I guess I can understand that. I'm sorry I spent the evening crying on your shoulder."

"Not the whole evening," he said. "And my shoulder is there for you anytime you want it."

Tristan popped his head between the seats, and Andrew scratched his head absently. "I was wondering if you'd like to go somewhere on Saturday? I have the whole day off."

"Where?"

"How about driving to Winnipeg?"

"Winnipeg! That's nearly a three-hour drive. What for?"

"I thought we could go for a nice dinner, maybe find a play or something to see."

"It's a long drive just for the day. I can't leave Tristan alone that long."

"We do have a terrific boarding kennel in Badger Lake," Andrew said with a grin.

"I still think Winnipeg is a little too far for a day trip."

"Well then, how about something simpler? We could go to a movie and then have a drink later."

"That sounds much better," said Taylor. "I'd like that. I

need to take my mind off things."

"I thought you might say it would be nice to have my company for the evening."

She blushed. "I'm sorry. I didn't mean it that way. Yes, I'd love to have your company for the evening."

"Nice save."

A loud squeal came over the radio and he answered it. Taylor couldn't quite connect the squawking words that came over, but thought she heard the words ambulance, garage, and Sandowski.

"Jenny's family?" she asked.

"Yep. I've got to go. I'll drop you on the way."

"That's all right. I'll get out here. We need to finish our walk anyhow."

As soon as she closed the door, Andrew swung the car around in a swirl of gravel and drove off.

She stared after the speeding car for a time before giving Tristan's leash a slight tug to start moving on. What could be wrong at Jenny's house? Would the police be called for a heart attack or something similar, or would they only send the ambulance for that?

She was nearly across town and a few blocks from home when she realized that in thinking about Jenny and the related problems, her mind had totally blocked out her conversations with her father. *Good!* That's what she wanted, a distraction. Then she felt guilty at that thought. Someone could have been in serious trouble, and she was happy about it? *Not your finest moment, Taylor.*

She knew, if she took a slight detour, she could have been within a block of Jenny's house, but she suppressed that thought immediately. Lookers just got in the way of emergency people, and it wasn't a situation where she should intrude. Heaven knew the Badger Lake hotline would have all the details in short order anyhow.

When she got home, Denver came over immediately to tell her he'd been ignored all day, and he was really starving. Taylor quickly flung down a bowl, opened a fresh tin of cat food, depositing about half of it in the bowl, and snapped a pink cover decorated with a picture of a cat's head on the rest. Both pets happy now, she flopped on the couch and turned on the television. Nothing good was on, but she couldn't concentrate anyhow.

On a whim, she snapped off the TV and grabbed her purse and jacket. "Not this time, old fellow," she said to an eager Tristan.

She walked the three blocks to Jack's real estate office. Just as she had her hand on the door, Jack came barrelling out, nearly knocking her over.

"Sorry," he called. "I have to run."

"Wait," she shouted after him. "Have you heard anything about Jenny?"

He didn't stop, merely waved a hand over his shoulder to signify he'd heard her but couldn't stop. He must have heard the news, whatever it was. Surely a meeting with a client wouldn't cause such a harried look as the one she'd seen while she was recovering her balance. Just how close were Jack and Jenny?

She walked past The Northland on the opposite side of the street and saw Edie coming from the other direction. She was still carrying the grocery bags she'd had when Taylor saw her earlier, but now they were full. It seemed forever since she'd talked to Edie that morning, but it was really only a couple of hours ago. Edie looked up and saw her, shifted the grocery bags she was carrying, and nodded in the direction of the restaurant. Taylor crossed the street and entered right behind her.

They sat at a table in the center of the restaurant this time. Taylor felt more comfortable where she could see who was sitting on all sides of her before starting a conversation. There was no need to be circumspect today. The restaurant was empty at the moment. Morning coffee was over, and it was just a little early for lunch.

They ordered coffee, and Taylor said, "Did you hear the ambulance?"

"Yes, it was headed to Sandowskis. Kevin has been away. I think it's just Jenny and the kids at home. I hope nothing's wrong with one of the boys."

Taylor nodded, then realized, by that logic, they were hoping something was wrong with Jenny, but she always preferred misfortunes not to fall on children.

"I went to see my father this morning." Taylor struggled with the term father and had momentarily considered calling him Des. That was the way she thought of him. She decided that was a little casual and settled back on simply the unemotionally descriptive father.

"Was it worth it?" asked Edie.

"I guess so. He told me what happened on the night he left. It wasn't a good enough excuse for disappearing totally from our lives. I'm sure he could have made contact if he'd really wanted to." She then went on to tell Edie the story as her father had related it. "Does it sound to you like what really happened?"

Edie fell silent for a moment, then said, "Yes, I think so. I never heard the whole story, of course, but from the bits and pieces I did catch, it matches with what I know."

"Did you ever know who the man was who was with my mother that night? My father called him Rod, said he was a friend of his, supposedly."

"Rodney Hainsworth."

Taylor looked up in amazement. "Really? Wasn't he Tara Leigh's father? You'd think I would have heard that since Tara Leigh spent so much time at our house with Greg. And my father said the man had left town with his family."

"They did, but came back a couple of years later. She came back first with Tara Leigh, and he followed her shortly afterward. That's maybe part of the reason Tara Leigh spent so much time with Greg and your family. Her parents had problems from the get-go, but I think their marriage really started to crumble after that night. They stayed married until they moved away this last time. They finally divorced a few years ago."

"What about the other man? The 'friend' Des said helped them get things sorted?"

Edie said slowly, "I'm not sure I should say since I'm not positive, but Grace always thought it was Terry Bingham. Your grandparents had the money to make things go away, but they needed someone to do the footwork. Terry needed money at the time, so it could have been him."

"Terry Bingham? Jenny's dad?"

"That's what Grace said."

"Don't you realize how that connects things?"

"I'm not exactly sure what you mean."

"My father. He's connected to Tara Leigh through her father, and he's connected to Jenny through her father. Don't you think that's a little too connected for comfort?"

"No, I certainly don't," said Edie firmly. "This is Badger

Lake. Everyone is connected one way or another. What are you thinking? That your father somehow is getting revenge on the children of the men he thinks did him wrong? That's ridiculous. Besides, we don't know yet that anything's the matter with Jenny. Maybe it was just an alarm gone off or some little household accident."

"Yes, I guess you`re right." Then another thought hit her. "Do you think my father could have been the burglar? Maybe he wanted to see if there was something incriminating in the attic that he should get rid of."

"You almost sound as though you want your father to be involved. Are you sure you're not trying to punish him for his absence by making him out to be the bad guy in everything else?"

"No! I'm not. I just think it's fair to consider everyone. That's all." She sat chewing on her bottom lip and then said, "Maybe I am angry at him, but it was a possibility. You have to admit that. It's quite a coincidence that he came back just when all the weird stuff started to happen."

"If you're going to bring up coincidences, what about Tara Leigh suddenly coming home? What about the two bur-glaries in the same house in a town that has practically no crime? What about everyone wanting to buy the house all of a sudden?"

"Okay, okay. I'll give my father a pass, for now at least. Besides," she added, "Tristan made friends with him, so he couldn't have been the second burglar." They sat in silence for a few minutes. Then Taylor asked, "Did you hear the am-bulance leave Jenny's house, or just arrive?"

"I think I heard the siren again, so that means someone was hurt. They wouldn't turn it on if they were just going back to the hospital empty. I'd better get these groceries home before my frozen peas start to melt." Edie stood up and gathered her purse and bags.

Taylor stood up to leave as well. They walked the first two blocks together without speaking. Then Edie turned to take the last block to her house.

"Call me if you hear anything," she said.

"With your connections, you're likely to hear before me," said Taylor.

"Oh, I don't know," said Edie with a smile. "You have a pretty good connection of your own."

"I don't think Andrew would tell me anything even if I asked. I'm sure he's not allowed to gossip in his job."

Edie grinned again and headed for home, leaving Taylor wondering about Andrew and just how closely connected they were. Should she continue to see him when she might be leaving Badger Lake shortly? But then, Andrew knew her plans to go. So she wasn't giving any false promises.

Chapter Ten

"Do you have the wagon?"

"Yes. And the key."

"No one saw you?"

"There's no one around. How would anyone know we were here? There's no lights, and the street ends at my house. I still don't think we should do this."

"We have to. You go ahead and make sure no one can see us. If you see anyone coming or watching, whistle and we'll hide till later."

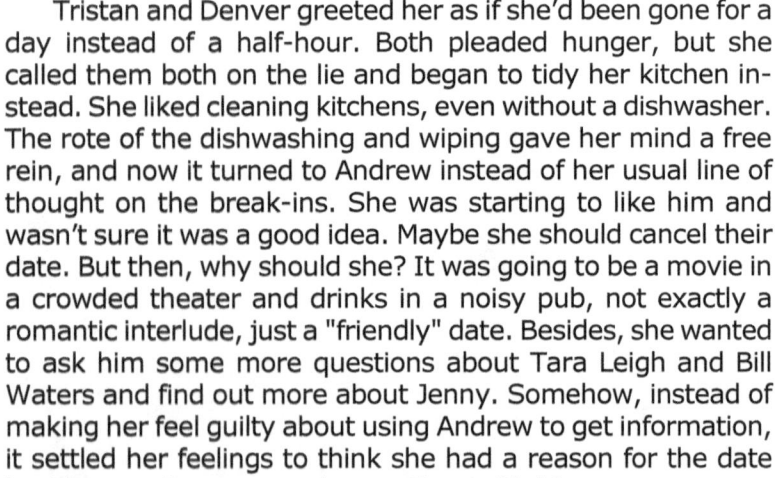

Tristan and Denver greeted her as if she'd been gone for a day instead of a half-hour. Both pleaded hunger, but she called them both on the lie and began to tidy her kitchen instead. She liked cleaning kitchens, even without a dishwasher. The rote of the dishwashing and wiping gave her mind a free rein, and now it turned to Andrew instead of her usual line of thought on the break-ins. She was starting to like him and wasn't sure it was a good idea. Maybe she should cancel their date. But then, why should she? It was going to be a movie in a crowded theater and drinks in a noisy pub, not exactly a romantic interlude, just a "friendly" date. Besides, she wanted to ask him some more questions about Tara Leigh and Bill Waters and find out more about Jenny. Somehow, instead of making her feel guilty about using Andrew to get information, it settled her feelings to think she had a reason for the date besides wanting to spend more time with him.

She made a tuna sandwich and a salad for lunch and had just finished eating the last bit of her sandwich under the accusing eye of her well-fed cat when she heard a knock on the door. She dropped the plate and cutlery into the sink and went to answer it.

She looked up into the serious face of Andrew, obviously in his working role, as he waited, unsmiling, for her to usher him in. He turned into the kitchen, another sign this was a business visit, but he accepted the coffee she handed him.

"What happened?" she asked, taking the chair across from him.

"Jenny's dead," he said simply.

"How?"

"She was in the garage in her car. It had run out of gas when we found her, but obviously it had been running with the door closed."

"It happened last night? But what about the boys?"

"The youngest boy, Jared, was away at a sleepover. The older one, Danny, thought his mother was sleeping in. He had breakfast before he finally went to look for her. The bed was made, but no sign of her. It was a lucky thing he started calling for her outside. A neighbor, Mrs. Donaldson, came to see what was going on, and she was the one to check the garage."

"Thank heavens for that. I imagine she'll have a hard time forgetting, though. Oh, those poor boys. What about her husband? Where was he?"

"He's out of town, supposed to be home tomorrow, but we got hold of him. He's on his way back now."

Andrew wiped a sheen of sweat from his forehead with his sleeved forearm. "You think bad things only happen in the big cities. I don't want to live through more days like this morning."

"It hits much closer when you know the people," Taylor agreed. "And then you realize what's going to face her family now."

Andrew had leaned back in his chair with the front legs raised, but now he set the chair down on all fours with a thump. "I have to ask you some questions, Taylor."

"Me?"

"You seem to be the common denominator in some of the things that have been going on around here."

"You seriously believe I had something to do with this?" Taylor could hardly get the words out. Shock, anger, and a little bit of fear combined to form a knot in her throat.

"I didn't say that. Have you talked to Jenny lately? If so, when and what about?"

"I talked to her a couple of times. She came over one night to ask me about selling the house. I told you about that," she said, glaring at him. "And I talked to her once more just the day before yesterday. No, it was yesterday."

"What about?"

"More of the same." Taylor flushed a little. "But we also talked about the break-ins I've had, Greg, Tara Leigh, and what happened to her."

"You were being nosy, in other words. Did she say anything?"

"Nothing new. She said Tara Leigh received a call, but they didn't know who from, and then she just went out. Do you think differently now about Tara Leigh's death?"

"Different how?"

"Different, as in, maybe it wasn't an accident."

"I never said I thought it was an accident."

"Yes, you did. I was the one trying to connect the dots."

Andrew corrected her. "I said the coroner decided it was an accident. Her husband is convinced it wasn't, and I have doubts."

"And Jenny?" she asked softly.

"It's too early to tell, and I can't really discuss more with you."

He stood up and picked up his hat from the table. "There's one thing more."

"There always is, *Columbo*," she said, trying to make a joke and realizing immediately it was a mistake.

"I don't think you should be staying here alone."

"Me? Whyever not?"

"Because, like I said, the strange things going on around here all seem to connect to you in some way. The break-ins, Tara Leigh coming to see you and then getting killed, your talks with Jenny." He ticked them off on his fingers as he spoke.

"My father arriving back suddenly," she added.

"In any case, I think you should either leave town for a few days, stay with someone, or maybe check into the motel till we know more about what is going on." His face softened as he added, "I really don't want anything bad to happen to you, Taylor."

"I'll think about it," she said. "But I have Tristan and Denver to worry about. Sooner or later, I'd just have to come back."

"Later would be better." Andrew turned to leave.

"Have you talked to Jack?" she asked.

"He's next," said Andrew. Before opening the door, he leaned over and kissed her softly on the forehead. "I don't usually do that with suspects," he said with a slight grin.

Taylor leaned against the door after Andrew left, feeling her pulse race. *A suspect? Does he really consider me a suspect?* She listened to the gravel crunch as his car pulled out of the driveway. She was pretty sure he was joking when he called her a suspect, but just the same, it must have been at the back of his mind or he would have never said it.

If she looked at the situation objectively, she supposed she'd have to consider herself on the list. She was connected either through herself or through Greg to everything that had happened. But then, if she was a suspect, why would she have robbed her own house and hurt her own dog? She relaxed as she thought along those lines. Of course, Andrew was joking. He would never have kissed her, taken her out, or asked her out again if he thought she were responsible for any of it.

Poor Jenny! Although she had never been an admirer of Jenny, it was awful to think of her dying that way. There was no way it could have been an accident, the way the coroner had dismissed Tara Leigh's death. And Taylor was pretty sure she would never have done it deliberately. Oh sure, Jenny had been having a few issues with her marriage, but she wasn't the kind to take her own life. She was more likely to lay the blame for her problems on other people. No way would she have killed herself in such a way that one of her boys would most likely be the one to find her. No mother could do that. And yet, Taylor read stranger things in the paper every day. She also remembered that scar on Jenny's wrist.

The tuna sandwich sat uncomfortably on her stomach. She had to either get some exercise or take a nap to get rid of that lump of nausea stuck inside her. She was too hyper and upset to try a nap, so a walk was the better option.

Tristan never objected to a walk. If she took him out twelve times in one morning, on the thirteenth he would be as eager to go as ever. He had a Jack Russell's unbounded energy and a short memory.

She stood for a bit by the back door, not sure where to go. She didn't want to walk past the Sandowski house or in the direction of the motel. She decided in the direction of downtown. She'd never thought to pick up her mail today, so she slipped back inside, grabbed her mail key, and set off with Tristan happily beside her.

The post office lobby was empty as she checked Grace's mailbox number 209. It was empty except for junk mail. Everyone that knew Grace knew she had died, and not much was getting forwarded to Taylor. Most of her correspondence was electronic.

She looked across the street and directly at the door of Jack's Badger Lakeland Real Estate office. She wondered if she dared see if she could talk to him today. He had been too busy to stop last time she saw him. Maybe it wasn't that he was too busy. She got the distinctive feeling he hadn't wanted to talk to her.

She should come to a decision soon about whether she was going to stay in Badger Lake or sell the house. She stopped. There it was again, the question of staying. Of course, she wasn't going to stay. But then, why did her brain increasingly toss the possibility at her when she least expected it? If she made the decision and actually listed the house, maybe her brain would shut up. Because there was no way she wanted to stay here. No way. And the way to make that clear to her annoying subconscious would be to list the house.

Jack wasn't her favorite person in Badger Lake, and she considered getting another agent, but he was the best known. As such, he had the best chance of selling the house.

She made the decision and, before she could change her mind, crossed the street. Just as she was about to open the door, Jack pushed it open from the other side. "What do you want?" he asked rather testily.

"I wanted to talk to you about the house," she said. "I think I'm going to list it, and I wanted to ask if you were still interested."

"If I sell your house for you, will you leave town?"

"Of course. That stands to reason." Jack's behavior was beginning to border on the bizarre.

"Come in." He motioned her to a navy blue, upholstered chair as he sat across from her at a large, expensive-looking desk from in a swivel chair. No offer of coffee or other amenities came. He opened a drawer and pulled out a form. He made no mention of Tristan, as though he were used to clients bringing their dogs along.

"All I need from you is what you want included in the sale and the amount you want. Everything else I can get myself, except for pictures. I'll have to come later and take some for the online listing." His tone hadn't mellowed.

"Have I done something to upset you?" Taylor asked.

"Not deliberately."

"Then why are you acting as though I'm something you'd call an exterminator to get rid of?"

He put down the form. "It's not personal, Taylor. You could be irritating when you were a kid, but I always thought of you as harmless. Now I'm not so sure."

"What do you mean?"

"Ever since you arrived back in town, there has been nothing but trouble."

"None of it was my fault," she protested. "Don't forget, it was my house that's been burglarized twice." She thought Jack twitched slightly at her protests, but went on. "I had nothing to do with Tara Leigh's death. I didn't even talk to her."

"She came back to town looking for you."

"How do you know that?"

He shrugged. "We kept in touch from time to time. She e-mailed me she was coming to see you."

"Well then, you must know why she wanted to talk to me."

"No." He snapped repeatedly at an elastic band on his wrist, and she noticed the small white scar there, just like Jenny's. She remembered Greg had one like that too. He had said he'd scratched it on a thorn. Strange, they were so similar.

"Why would she write to tell you she was coming to see me but not let you know why?"

"I don't know, Taylor." His voice held exasperation and something else, Taylor thought. Jack looked as though he had aged suddenly since she'd seen him just the other day. His eyes were bloodshot with pouches under them. His skin looked washed out, and his hands were jittery.

Could he be a secret drinker? No, that wouldn't explain the suddenness of the change. She didn't know why, but she swore he was afraid of something, and it felt like it could be her. Why?

"It's terrible what happened to Jenny," she said, watching for his reaction. "You were good friends, weren't you? I'm so sorry."

Jack threw his pen down on the desk. "Are you going to list the house with me or not, Taylor?" he half-yelled at her.

She stood up, Tristan jumping up to follow. "No, I think I've changed my mind, thanks. I'm going to fix it up instead. Then I'll decide what to do with it."

She glanced back at him as she walked out the door and saw him slump down in his desk, cradling his head in his hands. What in the world had come over him?

She was pretty sure Jack had been the burglar, especially from the way he'd twitched when she mentioned it. For some reason, he wanted his hands on Greg's journals, and it had to have something to do with Rebecca's disappearance all those years ago. That was the uniting factor for all the things that had happened, not Taylor. It was Rebecca.

She pulled at Tristan's leash as he tried to steer her in the direction of Merv's. Whenever he smelled food, he was obliged to check it out as though Taylor never fed him. She realized there was a flaw in her conclusion that Jack was the burglar. If he had hurt Tristan, surely the dog would have growled at him, but he'd shown no signs of animosity. That brought her back to her feeling that there were two different burglars. It was hard to fathom such an outbreak of crime in sleepy Badger Lake, but there was no other explanation. Jack had broken in the first time looking for the journals. The second break-in was someone else with the same goal in mind. And the only one Tristan had growled at was Bill.

By the time her mind had processed those thoughts, she was on her doorstep. Inside, she stepped on a note that had been thrust under her door. She smiled when she saw it was from Andrew. *"I'll pick you up tomorrow night at seven if that's all right."* He underlined the next words. *"Keep your door locked and the spare key inside. If you won't go stay with someone, at least be careful. You have my number. Call if anything unusual happens."*

Yes, Taylor had his number, but he also had hers. Why the note? Had the man never heard of texting or e-mail? She turned at the sound of a passing car. It was Andrew. He grinned and waved. So he had likely dropped by first and then scribbled the note when he found she wasn't home. She wasn't sure if that meant he was anxious for her company or if he still had niggling doubts about her position on the suspect list. In any case, his mood seemed to have improved. Maybe he was making progress on the case. But, was there a case? Maybe, against all odds, Jenny's death would turn out to be a suicide after all. Maybe Jenny had been depressed and had never considered the feelings of the people she had left behind. No, that idea didn't sit well. It didn't make sense. But then, she remembered the scar on her wrist. Could that relate to a previous attempt?

Taylor was barely inside when a knock came at the door. Andrew must have decided to come back. She opened the door with a smile on her face that quickly vanished. Des stood on the step.

"I take it from the smile you weren't expecting me?" he said, sliding into the room between her and the open door.

"You've got that right. What are you doing here?"

"We need to finish our conversation," he said, "especially in light of what's been happening."

She sighed and ushered him into the living room. "I thought we'd exhausted talk about anything we have in common."

"Not by a long shot. You didn't tell me this morning that the house had been broken into twice."

"It was none of your business. Besides—"

"Besides what?"

"I did wonder, for a moment, if it might have been you."

"Me! What would I want in this house?"

"You might have wanted to see if my grandparents left anything incriminating about you. If so, the attic would be the place to look."

"You said for a moment. What changed your mind?"

"Tristan." She pointed to where Tristan sat by her father's feet, chin resting across them as Des scratched him behind the ears. "The second time, whoever broke in, kicked Tristan. He wouldn't be so friendly if it had been you." Taylor was actually a little miffed that Tristan had taken to Des so easily. Weren't dogs supposed to sense your feelings? Shouldn't he know that Des wasn't exactly a welcome friend?

"That's not a problem anymore. I had a long talk with

Andrew, and he says I have nothing to worry about. The people who would have been chief witnesses against me are long gone, except for Rod and Terry, and I don't think either of them wants to rake it up again. Terry's still in town. I don't even know where Rod is."

"So why did you want to talk about the break-ins?"

"It's not just the break-ins. Look what's been happening in Badger Lake lately. This is a sleepy little town where nothing happens, and now we have burglaries—Tara Leigh going into the lake, and now, Jenny's dead. I just heard about her from some people at the motel."

"So?"

"I know I don't have any rights with you, but I'm still worried about you. You seem to be in the center of everything."

"So do you!"

"Me?"

"Yes," Taylor said. "Tara Leigh's father is the one who you beat up so badly. Jenny's dad is the one who helped get you out of town, and this house is still a place you lived for a while. You're connected as much as I am."

"There's one other person who was even more connected," said Des slowly.

"Who?" asked Taylor, knowing the answer but not wanting to hear it.

"Greg. He was best friends with both Jenny and Tara Leigh." He stopped to bend over and give Tristan a good stroking, then went on. "I told you I saw Greg when he was in rehab the last time. Well, I didn't tell you some of the things he said."

"Like what?"

"He was rambling a lot. I'm not sure if any of it was supposed to make sense, but he did talk about Jack, Jenny, Tara Leigh, and also Rebecca. I remember reading about her in the papers when she disappeared. For some reason, Greg seemed to feel as though he should have stopped whatever happened to make her go away. He was mumbling about 'old shadows never letting light in.' I wasn't sure what he meant, but I think it's related to Rebecca, and I think it's also got something to do with what's happening now."

Taylor hated to admit that she felt the same, but she nodded. "I'm sure Greg knew where Rebecca went, but I've never been able to figure out why he wouldn't tell anyone, to stop all the hurting that went on."

"That brings us to Bill Waters," said Des.

"I'm pretty sure he was the one who broke into the house, at least the second time. When I was walking Tristan, we ran into the Waters, and he stopped and growled. I had to drag him away. Evelyn made some comment about dogs never liking Bill, but it was more than that. Tristan's hackles were up."

"Have you told Andrew all of this?"

She nodded. "Well, most of it anyway. I think he's working along the same lines. I know he was going to talk to Jack. Maybe he can shed some light on things. Jack sure won't talk to me."

Des stood. Taylor realized she was almost sorry to see him go. Then she thought back to twenty years of silence and gave him a curt goodbye on the step. As she closed the door with a little more force than necessary, the phone rang. The land line meant it was probably Edie. It was.

"I wanted to let you know I had a strange phone call a while ago," said Edie.

"Not weird phone calls, too? What's happening in Badger Lake?"

"Not that kind of strange phone call. I mean an unusual one, not a heavy breathing one. It was from Jack."

"Jack? Well, I had a strange visit with him earlier."

"I know. That's why he called me. He seems to think I have some pull with you and wants me to convince you to leave town."

"What is going on with that man? He acted so bizarrely when I went to talk to him. I thought he wanted to buy the house, and I was actually considering selling it through him. Then he started to vent at me, and I just left. Has he always been a little paranoid, or is that a recent thing?"

"As long as I've known Jack, he's been outgoing and friendly, just as you'd expect from someone whose business is selling. It's definitely a recent thing, this strange behavior."

"He wants me out of town so badly, and I don't know the reason. I thought I was the sinned against person here, not the sinner, but Jack seems to think I'm responsible for all the bad things happening."

"Don't you think his actions are those of a man with a

guilty conscience?"

"Perhaps, but guilty of what? He could have been my in-truder, at least the first one, but that's not enough guilt to cause his reaction. I still think it has something to do with Rebecca. Maybe he had some responsibility with whatever happened to her, and my coming back has made him fright-ened of it coming out."

"That would make sense." Edie paused a moment before continuing. "I think maybe you're right about it relating to Rebecca. But that means, if Jack is connected, it is likely Tara Leigh and Jenny are also."

"And Greg. Isn't that what you're trying to say?"

"I'm sorry, Taylor, but I think it has to be that way. Re-becca went missing and everyone involved has suddenly started showing up or changing behavior. I think your com-ing back is the trigger."

Taylor sighed. "I know. I've pretty much come to the same conclusion. That brings us back to Bill Waters. I'm sure he's the one who broke in. Tristan growled at him. He must have some idea of what happened all those years ago, and, if it was him who took the journals, there must have been something in there to confirm it."

"What does Andrew think?"

"He wouldn't tell me, I'm sure. I know he talked to Jack, and he definitely thinks Tara Leigh's death is not an accident."

"Well, maybe you can get something more from him to-morrow tonight. Let me know. I have to run." Taylor heard Jasper barking in the background as Edie hung up.

Taylor grinned. Badger Lake didn't need a gossip column in the paper. They only needed to call Edie. She knew what everyone was doing. How had she heard about Taylor's date with Andrew?

Then her grin died. If she and Edie had read things right, and if Tara Leigh's death wasn't an accident, did that mean Bill Waters was taking some sort of revenge for his daugh-ter? Or could her death be unrelated to the rest? Maybe Tre-vor had his own reasons to follow his wife to Badger Lake. And what had Tara Leigh wanted to talk to her about? It had to be something to do with Greg. And, since his behavior had changed so radically too, the only connecting factor had to be Rebecca.

Chapter Eleven

They parted at the corner, the wagon now at the nui-sance grounds under a pile of debris.

"We have to get rid of it. Say you lost it."

"But why?"

"Don't you ever watch television? They have forensics and stuff that can find things."

"Sh. Lights."

They ducked behind some shrubbery till the car passed.

"Do you think anyone saw us?"

"How? We're on the edge of town. No one drove by that we didn't see first and hide from. Your aunt is on the other side of the house watching TV. Those big trees hide all the other houses."

"We'd better get home. We don't want to be late. Then people will start asking questions."

"I was supposed to be home half an hour ago."

"When did you ever follow curfew? They won't be worried."

"One more thing. We have to swear a blood oath we won't say a word to anyone."

"That's kid stuff."

"We have to do it. I'll go first."

Strangely, Taylor slept well that night. She had expected to lie awake, mulling over events, but from the moment Tristan and Denver curled up at her feet until she felt the sun on her face in the morning, she was dead to the world.

She went for her morning walk with Tristan, deciding to

let the past have a rest for a bit. After all, it was Andrew's job to solve the problems. Soon, she would put the house on the market with the other real estate agent and be out of Badger Lake forever and back to her normal life. Somehow, that thought didn't seem as comforting as it should. In spite of the unpleasant happenings, she sensed a growing attachment to the town of her childhood. She remembered the good times with Aunt Grace and Greg as they grew up. She liked the familiarity of the streets and gardens. She enjoyed the growing friendship with Edie. There was also Andrew. She would miss him when she left. Maybe she hadn't been too smart to date a man she knew would never be part of her life. After tonight, she resolved she wouldn't agree to see him anymore. Maybe he would even cancel their movie date if he was busy.

Late afternoon, her cell rang. The caller ID showed it was Andrew. "Hello, you."

"Hello, yourself. Just checking to make sure we're still on for that movie tonight?"

"Sure, if you still want to."

"You don't sound thrilled about the idea. Has something happened?"

"I thought maybe you'd be busy with Jenny and everything. I'd been expecting you to call and cancel."

"Nope. There's not much more I can do at the moment except catch up on my paperwork, which I'm doing now. Early show starts at seven-thirty. Then maybe we can catch a drink and a bite at the pub?"

"Okay. See you then." She snapped her cell shut and stared down at Tristan who was looking at her inquiringly. "Sorry, old chap. You and Denver are on your own tonight. Let's get your dinners, and then I can figure out what to wear to a movie in Badger Lake."

She couldn't remember what was listed on the billboard, even though she'd walked past the theater more than once, and there was no paper to check the listings. Hopefully, it wasn't a wild cop show. She didn't even know what Andrew's tastes were in movies. Or in anything, come to think of it.

He picked her up a few minutes early, but she was ready. Taylor had never been a last minute wardrobe changer. She said goodbye to Tristan and Denver, ignoring their accusing expressions and was out the door before Andrew had a chance to knock.

The movie was a comedy, not a bad one. It felt good to release her emotions with some laughter. As they filed out of the movie theater with the other few dozen viewers, Andrew's cell phone rang. No fancy downloaded tones for him, just a simple ring. He stopped and, glancing at the call display, stepped over to the privacy of the side wall to answer. She stood, waiting and wondering what new disaster was in the wind. From the expression on Andrew's face, it wasn't a personal call.

"I'm sorry, the drink will have to wait for another night," he said as he took her arm and guided her to the car. "I'll have to drop you home."

"Problems?"

"It was Jack. He sounded off the wall. Says he needs to talk to me urgently."

"He's been off the wall for the last couple of days," said Taylor as Andrew reversed the car out of the angle parking spot. "He as much as accused me of being responsible for all that's happened in Badger Lake, and he called Edie yesterday to ask her to convince me to leave town."

"He didn't mention you, but he thinks someone is out to get him. Apparently, his brakes went out on his car, and he thinks someone tampered with them." He looked over at her. "I shouldn't be talking to you about this. Don't repeat any of it."

Taylor gave him an offended look. "Who would I repeat it to?"

"Well, to Edie for a start." He grinned. "But you don't really need to tell her anything. She usually knows it all."

Taylor smiled. "Usually true, but it doesn't seem to be working this week. She's as much in the dark as everyone about what's happening. At least, I think she is," Taylor amended. Maybe Edie knew more than she was telling her.

Andrew dropped her at her door and sped off. *What does Jack want now?* wondered Taylor. Maybe his panic was more than the guilty conscience she and Edie had imagined. If they were right about the connection of the deaths of Jenny and Tara Leigh, then maybe Jack had good reason to worry. She thought of the manic personality of Bill Waters and double checked the locks on her doors. She wasn't going to risk intruders tonight.

Then she realized Tristan still needed his final pee of the night and let him out into the backyard to do his business. With a twinge of fear raising the hairs on the back of her neck, she slipped back into the kitchen while Tristan ran around the yard. She reached into the junk drawer, looking for added security. She pulled out an old hammer. It would make her feel more secure sitting on the night table. She nearly laughed at her fears. It was Jack who might have reason to worry, not her. Yet it was here she'd been victimized by a burglar twice. Still, they'd gotten what they wanted. She shouldn't have anything to fear now.

The kitchen light went out as Tristan began a frenzied barking in the backyard. "Stupid bulb. I should have replaced them all with the new energy-saving ones." She slipped into the living room, fumbling in the dark to turn on one of the table lamps for another light as Tristan ran into the house barking as though the banshees from hell were after him. Now she was seriously alarmed. How had he gotten into the house? She had left the back door closed.

"Don't bother turning it on," came a chilling voice behind her. Evelyn's voice had a deadly edged tone to it. "There's enough light in here for me to do what I came for."

Now that her eyes were becoming accustomed to the darkness, she could see Evelyn's profile take shape in the darkness, along with the shotgun she held in front of her pointed toward Taylor.

Tristan stopped his barking and began to growl, a low rumble in his throat.

"Shut the dog up or I'll take care of him properly this time."

Taylor called Tristan in a shaky voice and kept her hand on his head as she spoke a few soothing words to him. She hoped they would calm him more than they were calming her.

"You came back and stirred the pot properly, didn't you?" said Evelyn grimly. "Too bad your worthless brother isn't here to take his just desserts. Well, you'll have to stand in for him."

"I don't understand."

"Oh, I think you understand perfectly," said Evelyn. "I knew all those years ago your brother had something to do with Rebecca going missing. I knew she would never go away and leave us wondering. I knew he was responsible."

"He wasn't. I'm sure of it. Greg liked Rebecca. He wouldn't have done anything to harm her."

"Rebecca thought he was her friend. She used to talk about him like he was a hero or something. But he wasn't, was he? He let that Tara Leigh bitch torment Rebecca and didn't try to stop it."

"He did. He did. He talked about it in the journal. He tried to make Tara Leigh be nice to Rebecca. He thought she'd decided to be friends with her."

"Friends? Some friends. I expected it of them." She nearly spat the words. "But Rebecca deserved more from Greg. She trusted him. He let her down. And now, someone has to pay."

She shifted the gun slightly and Taylor tensed, knowing she had to play for time. Surely someone would have heard Tristan barking. Someone might notice the back door open. Someone...Andrew! He was talking to Jack. He probably guessed what had happened by now. He'd come back to check on her.

"Was it in the journals?" Taylor asked, wanting Evelyn to keep talking, sensing, in spite of her bad intentions, she wanted to talk it out, to justify her actions.

"The journals? They were useless."

"What made you look for them?"

"That day at the post office you said you'd had an intruder upstairs in the attic. I knew then it was one of Greg's friends. You were telling everyone you were going to fix the house up and sell it. You said the journals were in the attic. We all heard it. That's why they broke in. I knew then that Rebecca was buried somewhere, and they all knew. Greg kept a journal. That's why they all acted so strange. They were afraid of what he'd written. I thought it was that Tara Leigh bitch that broke in. I wanted to get the journals from her and find out where my Rebecca was buried."

"You were the one who phoned her."

"I told Bill I had a headache and to go to the prayer meeting without me. I told him I took one of my pills, the strong ones the doctor gave me to sleep. Then I took that bottle of his with me. I knew she'd been a drinker once, and I could use it."

"How did you get her to drive into the lake?"

"It wasn't that hard. I called her and told her I'd found some old letters Rebecca had written, and one was to her. I told her it was unopened and asked if she wanted it. Of course, the stupid woman believed me. I even gave her a chance. I asked her for the journals. She pretended she didn't know what I was talking about. Stupid cow. I asked her and asked her about what happened that night. Then she laughed at me and said she was leaving. I grabbed her and hit her head against the door of the car, and she went limp. Then I poured that bottle of Bill's down her throat till she gagged and wouldn't swallow any more. By then, she wasn't saying much of anything, just whimpering like the pathetic creature she was. I gunned the car through the driver's door and aimed it at the lake. It rolled slowly and kind of slipped over the bank. Luckily, it was deep there. I watched to make sure she didn't get out, and then I went home."

"But the journals?" Taylor insisted. "It must have been you the second time. You kicked Tristan. That's why he growled. It wasn't at Bill. It was at you."

"I got the journals for all the good they did me. There was nothing in there. On the day after they killed Rebecca, he just made a short entry. *Rebecca is gone now. I'll miss her. If only Tara Leigh could have been her friend.*" Her voice rose now. "That's all he said after they murdered my baby."

"They wouldn't have murdered her. Whatever happened, it must have been an accident."

"That's not what Jenny said."

"Jenny told you what happened?" In spite of the fear that gripped Taylor, she wanted to know. She wanted to know how Greg fit in the story. She needed to know what had caused him the torment that threw him into seeking refuge in chemicals.

"They were so afraid of anyone finding out what they'd done to my girl. When I called Jenny and told her I had a letter, she was just like Tara Leigh. She couldn't wait to get her hands on anything that might make her look bad. She invited me for coffee after the kid was in bed. So, I took my little pills, and when she wasn't looking, I doctored her coffee. I was able to get her to the garage so the boy wouldn't wake and hear us. I tried to get her to tell me where they put Rebecca. She said the lake, but I know she lied."

"What makes you think she lied?"

"Because they wouldn't have been so worried about you fixing up the house if Rebecca wasn't here somewhere. And those kids, how could they have gotten her to the lake? They don't have a car."

"I guess you're right. But I still think Greg would have had no part of it."

"He was the worst of all. He was the one Rebecca trusted. He was the one who betrayed her. He should have stopped them."

"Maybe he tried." She took a gulp as Evelyn moved a step closer. The gun was so close she could almost reach out and touch it. What if she did? Was there any hope Evelyn might be distracted long enough for her to make a lunge for it? Her best bet was to keep Evelyn talking and wait for a moment of inattention, then grab the gun. But Evelyn was too focused.

"Did Jenny say how Rebecca died?"

"All she said over and over was that it was an accident. They didn't do it. She fell. But, by then, she was going to sleep so I couldn't make out anything else she said."

"So you put her in the running car and locked the garage door?" *Slow down, Taylor. She's nearly at the end of her story. You should delay it, not hurry her along.*

"I made a mistake. Now I may never know what happened. I should have kept her awake longer."

"You sabotaged Jack's car, too, didn't you?"

"Yes. He'll not be telling any stories now." Then she jerked the gun and said, "How did you know about Jack?"

"I was with Andrew when he called."

"He called? That means I didn't do it right."

"How could you know he'd have an accident? What if he discovered his brakes wouldn't work?"

"I called him to look at a property out past the big hill." *Such a busy woman on the phone*, thought Taylor. Why did no one recognize her voice? "He wouldn't have a chance on that big hill. The brakes must have gone too soon or too late. I used to go to the garage when I was a girl and watch my father. I learned a lot. I loved it. If I'd been a boy, I would have been a mechanic." Then she tightened her grip on the gun. "We've talked enough. It's time for you to take Greg's punishment."

Taylor braced to make a move for the gun when she saw

a shadowy figure behind Evelyn. She gasped, and the sound made Evelyn turn just enough for Taylor to make a grab for the shotgun. One of the barrels went off as she heard the newcomer say, "Evelyn, what have you done?" She recognized Bill's voice.

Taylor made one last pull and the gun clattered to the floor. She couldn't see where it landed and took off running out the front door, Tristan now yapping at her heels, released from his enforced silence.

She heard another explosion. That meant the gun was empty for now, so Taylor was going to be sure she was far away before it could be reloaded. She ran into the street. She heard a siren very close by, and the lights of a fast car turned the corner. Taylor jumped to the side as Andrew sped up. He jumped out of the car before it had completely stopped and ran toward the house.

"Evelyn?" he asked her as he ran.

"And Bill. They're both there," she shouted back.

"Stay here." It was one command Taylor intended to obey.

Footsteps announced the arrival of more people. Des came running from the back alley behind the house, and Edie was not far behind him, hindered by her bad knee. Where was everyone coming from? Soon the whole town would be here.

"What are you doing here?" Taylor demanded.

It was Edie who answered. "Des came to talk. He was worried something bad was going to happen to you, and he wanted me to come and get you."

She looked at Des, and he shrugged. "I knew you wouldn't listen to me," he said. "I thought maybe Edie could keep you safe."

"Then we called Andrew," Edie went on. "But he was already on his way over. I guess he had it all figured out without our help."

"I'm glad he had it right. I was so sure all along it was Bill. I never thought of Evelyn."

The lights went on in the house and Andrew appeared in the doorway, waving them in.

Inside the house, he steered them into the kitchen. "You don't want to go in there," he said, jerking his head toward the living room. She heard another siren coming closer. "That will be the ambulance," Andrew said, "but they won't be able to do anything."

Bill Waters sat at Taylor's kitchen table, a sight she never thought she'd see. He appeared to have shriveled even more than usual and his face was ashen. It was the first time she had seen him totally still. He seemed to be in a near trance.

Taylor looked at Andrew and then at the living room. He shook his head. Taylor didn't know if that meant not to walk inside or that there was no hope for Evelyn, maybe both. He went to open the door for the emergency crew.

Taylor did the only thing she could think of to keep busy. She put on the kettle. Bill looked like he needed something for shock, and they could all do with a restorative cup of tea.

In a few moments, she heard the door close again and assumed Evelyn was gone. Andrew came in as she was trying to hand Bill a cup of tea. He seemed to be unaware of her or her offer. Then Andrew put his arm around Bill's shoulders and said, "Drink this." He held out the cup and Bill took a tentative sip, then crumpled into a fit of weeping.

Taylor couldn't think of anything useful to do. She desperately wanted to get out of the confined kitchen, but she couldn't face passing the living room. Edie and Des seemed to be as uncertain as she. Andrew gently urged Bill to his feet and guided him to the door. "Call Dr. McPhee," he said. "I'm going to get him to the hospital. Go to Edie's, all of you. I've got to seal off the house till I can get a forensics unit here. I'm going to leave Jason here for the time being." He gestured to the young policeman who had materialized in the doorway.

As usual, Edie seemed to know the number to call. Then, with a nod from Jason, they started to leave. "Can I just get some things from the bedroom?" asked Taylor. He nodded again, not a talkative sort, but then no one was in the mood for conversation. She skirted the entry to the living room, trying not to look in, and quickly ran up the stairs.

It didn't take her long to grab a change of clothes. Tristan followed, not letting her out of his sight for a minute. "My cat's still here," she said to Jason. "Don't let him get out. You can shut the kitchen door to keep him in here away from..." Her voice trailed off. "I've just got to check his food and water."

When they left the house, Taylor realized Des had left without word. She was almost sorry he had gone, not because she wanted his company, of course, but she wanted to ask a lot of questions. She was too tired tonight to concentrate anyhow. She'd see him tomorrow.

Edie's place felt like home, the amount of time she was spending there. She wondered if she'd ever feel safe in her house again. Edie started to put the kettle on, but Taylor stopped her. "I think we need this more than we need tea," she said, brandishing a bottle of wine. "I grabbed it when I was getting my clothes. I don't know about you, but I'm going to need something to get me off to sleep tonight."

Chapter Twelve

He lay behind the dumpster in the alley, curled up in a fetal position, shivering in the night wind as he held oblivion in his grasp. His hands shook, then steadied with intense concentration as he shot the needle home. "I'm so sorry, Rebecca," he muttered. "It was all my fault. I should have stopped it. All my fault."

Taylor woke later than usual. She felt groggy, but luckily, she had no wine headache. There was no sign of Tristan. Edie must have given him his morning romp in the back yard with Jasper. She heard Edie knocking about in the kitchen. She took a quick shower and headed downstairs.

"Breakfast is ready," said Edie. "I think this morning calls for a proper meal. It's not going to be a pretty day."

Taylor felt a little nauseous at the first whiff of bacon, but her stomach quickly decided it was hungry, and she managed to polish off her plate. They ate silently. Edie called the dogs in, and Taylor began the dishes.

Before they had a chance to start dissecting yesterday's events, there was a knock at the door.

Andrew said, "I'm glad you're up. I hate to bother you, but you have to know, Taylor. We need to dig out that old well in the backyard."

Taylor paled. "Is that where..."

"Yes. Can I come in for a minute?"

Taylor poured him some coffee and refilled her cup. Edie sat down at the table as well.

"Did Jack tell you that's where Rebecca is?"

"Yes. When he called me last night, Jack was terrified. His car brakes failed. It was lucky he wasn't speeding or on the big hill when they went. He stopped without problems and called me. He said someone was out to get them all. He was pale and shaking. He couldn't even drive home."

"He guessed who it was?"

"Like you, he thought it was Bill, because he was the one who was all mouth and always talking about God's punishment for wrongdoers. No one thought it could be Evelyn. Everyone felt sorry for her, losing her daughter and then having to put up with Bill on top of that."

"I was so sure it was Bill," said Taylor. "When Tristan growled on my walk the other day, I thought it meant that Bill was the burglar. Evelyn threw in that comment about dogs not liking Bill. I never dreamed it was her."

"Well, at least you had the rest of it right," said Andrew. "It all went back to Rebecca's disappearance. Jack told me about the night she died. He wanted to get it off his chest."

"It was an accident, though, wasn't it?"

Andrew shrugged. "Maybe a preventable accident."

"Can you tell us what Jack said?"

"Not really. For one thing, I don't know how much he colored the story to put the blame on Tara Leigh, but it comes down to a severe case of bullying and taunting Rebecca into doing something dangerous. Oh, what the heck. Everyone in town will know anyway. They were in the old creamery, and there were some high beams. Jenny did a little dance across them. She was a gymnast. Then Tara Leigh goaded Rebecca into it. She was scared, fell, and hit her head. She was dead. The kids knew they'd be blamed, so they put her in the wagon Greg used for paper deliveries and brought her to the old shed. They dragged the lid off the old well, put her in, and sealed it tight again."

"Wouldn't we have noticed an...odor?" asked Taylor.

"Probably not. It was sealed tightly. And Grace does have a compost heap out there. It would get the blame."

Taylor felt sick. The bacon was sitting very uneasily in her stomach. So that's why Greg spent his life in a torment of guilt. If only he had told someone. If only one of them had told. Besides Rebecca, three more people were dead and a few more lives shaken.

"How's Bill?"

I haven't seen him yet. The doc has him doped up, and I think it will take some therapy to get him in any sort of a normal state."

"He was always a little strange. This might really push him off the deep end. So, when he and Evelyn were struggling with the gun, and I heard it go off, it actually killed her?"

"Yes. She was dead when I got inside."

"Will Bill be charged?"

"I doubt it. It was an accident. He'd be in no fit state to be charged anyhow. There will be a hearing, of course."

"And Jack?"

"Not up to me. I just collect the information. Rebecca's death was an accident, but what they did afterwards...I don't know. It was a long time ago, and they were just kids. It will be up to the crown representatives of Her Majesty." He stood up. "And now I have to go. I think you'll want to stay here another day, till we're finished with your yard."

Chapter Thirteen

Taylor covered the salad and checked the oven to be sure the lasagna was on schedule. Hearing Tristan give a happy bark in the backyard, she checked to see what mischief he might have found. His bark was directed across the fence toward the kennels where Edie was returning three dogs to their runs.

Taylor had been too busy with her renovations to talk to Edie much over the last week, so she leaned across the fence. "I see you've decided to go ahead with the boarding?"

"On a casual basis," said Edie. "I don't know how much business I'll do, or even how much I want to do, but these three belong to a family out at the lake. They decided taking three dogs on a fishing trip wasn't such a good idea."

She closed the kennel door and gestured toward Taylor's backyard. "I see the shed is gone."

"That was first on my list of priorities. I couldn't stand the thought of looking out there and thinking about the well. And about Rebecca and Jenny and Tara Leigh..." Her voice trailed off.

"How about the house?"

"Well, Jimmy says the roof is in good shape, so that's a bonus."

"The shingles were new after the big hailstorm two years ago."

"Oh yes, I forgot about that. Anyhow, I'm going to have some painting done inside and the kitchen refitted, but that's about it for now. I'm not going to have any walls torn down or anything."

"I don't see a sale sign on the lawn."

"Well," said Taylor, a little sheepishly after all her protes-tations about leaving Badger Lake. "I'm not sure I'm going to sell, at least not yet."

"Ah," said Edie.

"I thought maybe I could reconnect to Greg here. I mean the old Greg, the way he was before Rebecca died. We had some good times in Badger Lake. It wasn't a bad childhood at all. I think I blamed Badger Lake somehow for the change in Greg. That's why I stayed away."

"Greg had a more demanding conscience than the others. I think that's why he couldn't live with what they did."

"I know the world is full of 'if onlys,' but if only..."

"Have you seen Des?" Edie asked after a reflective pause.

"I talked to him a couple of times before he went back home."

"Are you going to keep in touch?"

"I don't know. Maybe. Probably. I can't quite forgive him for deserting us all those years, but I've found out people can get so caught up in events that it changes their behavior. Maybe we'll exchange e-mails once in a while."

"I thought maybe another person had a part to play in your decision to stay." She nodded her head to Taylor's driveway where Andrew was getting out of the car, holding a large bundle of flowers.

"Oh," said Taylor. "I'm cooking him dinner tonight. I fig-ure I owe him that since I misjudged him. I thought he was ignoring what happened to Tara Leigh and Jenny. But he wasn't."

Andrew lifted his arm in greeting to them both, holding the flowers aloft.

"Nothing beats flowers," said Edie with a grin. "I do like a good, old-fashioned man."

About the Author

Sharon McGregor is a west coast transplant from the Canadian prairies. Her imagination and story weaving got its start when she was an only child living on a farm. She's moved on from cowgirl dreams to romance and mystery, but hasn't lost her love for horses.

She has moved to Vancouver Island to escape prairie winters but still can be found at ice arenas watching her grandchildren play hockey and figure skate. When not fighting for control of the keyboard with her cat Zoey she is running a business she shares with her daughter.